RIPENING

THE CONCLUSION TO THE ERIKA FROHMANN SERIES

VALERIE TAYLOR

B
B

BANNED BOOKS
Austin, Texas

A BANNED BOOK

FIRST EDITION

Copyright © 1988
By Valerie Taylor

Published in the United States of America
By Edward-William Publishing Company
Number 231, P.O. Box 33280, Austin, Texas 78764

ISBN 0-934411-10-7

Other Books By Valerie Taylor

The original Erika Frohmann series:
• *Journey To Fulfillment*
• *World Without Men*
• *Return To Lesbos*

Also by Valerie Taylor:
• *Prism*

These books are available from your bookseller or through the mail from
Naiad Press, P.O. Box 10543, Tallahassee, Florida 32302.

ONE

The telephone was ringing. Erika dropped her briefcase, turned the key, pushed the door open, and got there before it stopped. "Hello? Hello?"

"Miss Frohmann? Erika?"

"Isabel?" Erika's forehead puckered. I've been her grandmother's lover for more than twenty years and she still doesn't know what to call me. Well, be fair, the kid never heard of me until six months ago and she hasn't been exactly eager to get acquainted. It's hard for her, too. She said neutrally, "What's on your mind?"

"Can I come over for a little while after dinner?"

"Come *for* dinner." There was no warmth in Erika's voice, it was only courteous. "We can take something out of the freezer."

"No, after is better. Around nine?"

"Make it eight. Frances has a full day tomorrow."

"All right." Isabel hung up without a goodbye, Erika replaced the handset on the hall table and went back to collect her belongings and shut out the desert heat. Time for a shower before she started cooking. The thermometer said 107, Fahrenheit.

She felt prickly. Isabel's previous visits, both of them, had left her feeling divided between guilt and resentment; not all of the resentment was on Frances's behalf. Let the kid accept us or ignore us, she had thought. Her mother's attitude was better; Mari, corporation wife and bridge player, suburban housewife, and political helpmate, had pretended for more than two decades that her husband's mother didn't exist. She had probably been politely rude and self-seeking at nineteen.

She had changed her clothes but not her mood, and was chopping onions on a cutting board when Frances drove in,

1

parked under the carport, and came in through the kitchen door. "What a day! What are we having for supper?"

"The rest of the ham scalloped with potatoes. What do you mean, what a day? Good or bad?" If she's too tired, I'll call the dorm and tell Isabel not to come. Why should she intrude on our time together, anyway?

"The Reinert kid walked without his crutches. That Grijalva is one hell of a surgeon."

"You did it too. How many times have you come home aching from the massage? How many times did you talk to the kid? Anyway it should have been you in there with the little saws and pliers and stuff."

"Don't be ridiculous. And don't worship surgeons. Just because I'd have liked to be one, if I'd started earlier — what I do is important too." Frances ran a glass of tap water and drank it thirstily. Erika said, as she so often did, "There's cold in the fridge," and got the standard answer. "No, I like it room temp."

"How long do you suppose this stuff will hold out? The level's getting lower every year. The Jacobsens were watering their yard when I got home, third time this week." It was a delaying tactic, and she knew it.

"The Jacobsens will be the first to yell when the rates go up. Ought to last our time anyhow, unless the gov gets honest and gives the Indians their fair share." Erika swept the onions into a pottery bowl and looked out across the patio, planted with straggly cacti. She laid an onion-scented hand against Frances' cheek. "I know what you do is important. It's just that I'd like to see you get some of the credit."

Frances said dreamily, "You know, this is my favorite room."

"More than the bedroom?"

"I'm talking about form, not function. Maybe we could get to bed early for a change."

Erika took a deep breath. It couldn't be put off any longer. "Isabel called. She's coming over at eight. I asked her for dinner," Erika said, a little defensively, "I figured we could break out the frozen pizza, but she thought she'd rather come later. If the food in commons is anything like it used to be —"

Frances began unbuttoning her shirt. "Time for a shower before your casserole's done? It was a hundred and eight at noon." Her uniform slacks fell to the floor. "Sometimes I wonder why the kid came to see us in the first place. Or why they landed here in Tucson, for that matter. Of course the company shifted Bob out here, he didn't know where I was, he probably had no intention of going into politics. It's a whole series of happenstances. Why is he sending Isabel to the U, if it comes to that? Smith or Vassar would be more Mari's style."

"Politics. If you're running for a seat in the state legislature, you support the state university."

"Lucky for him I took back my own name when I got the divorce. There aren't too many Ollenfields around." Frances was naked now, sturdy but still slender, the late-afternoon sunlight dappling her body. She bent to scoop up her discarded clothes, but lingered. "You know, I was in Bob's house just one time after he married. Courtesy dinner, you have to be polite to the in-laws even if he's a drunk and she's a dyke. Mari was the perfect little *Ladies Home Journal* hostess. I mean she knew the score, I'd been in police court the day of the wedding, but she'd have died sooner than admit it. After I left Bill they never made any effort, not the least effort to find out where I was."

"The kid came to see you after she found out where you were." Why am I defending her, Erika wondered. She's no kin of mine.

"With a nice impersonal present from a gifty shoppy. Like, what do you give a grandmother you've just met? I don't care, you know."

Erika bent to open the oven door. What in the Goddess' sweet name made me start all this? "You better get your shower. It's after six."

She was putting plates on the table when Frances reappeared in shorts, her hair wet, her feet bare. "I must say you don't look much like a grandmother."

"No blonde rinse, no support hose? You know, it occurs to me that we're sort of old-fashioned, you and me. I've tried pot a few times, but it never did anything for me—don't want anything stronger because I don't like to feel my mind slipping—

don't even take one drink since my blood pressure went up. Don't go out much nights, unless it's symphony. I don't even want an open-ended relationship—hah, whose end? Isabel's generation thinks monogamy is a sin, they're just as hidebound as my great-grandmother."

"So maybe they get a thrill out of breaking their own rules," Erika said, not very interested. They had been over all this a dozen times, they were basically in agreement, so why keep bringing it up? "What amazes me is this swing to celibacy. I can understand it, there's nothing like overeating to make you want to diet, but how long can they keep it up?"

"Gives them another rule to break." Frances helped herself to salad and handed the bowl across the table. The savory ham and potatoes were sharpening her appetite. "It's a different world. Our restrictions were laid on us from outside. Isabel and her crowd can ignore the churches and the Moral Majority—we might have defied them, but we couldn't have ignored them." She took a big bite, cogitating. "Maybe the straight women will all die from the IUD and the Pill, and the men will give in to AIDS, and we dykes will inherit the earth."

"For a woman who won't even step on a black widow spider—"

"I'm not wishing, I'm just prophesying." Fran sighed. "You know, I never want to leave the desert. I thought you were crazy for wanting to come out here, but it sort of grows on a person. I know how the Indians feel about their land—it's holy, they don't want to part with it. Even when it's a hundred and ten in the shade and all the shade is over in Maricopa County."

I like Arizona. I like Tucson, even if we never get enough sidewalks. It's a great big, overgrown village."

"Erika, have you ever been sorry? About us, not about coming here."

"Only when you ask dumb questions, or when you talk like the millennium's here. There's a bill before Congress right now withholding funds from any organization that supports gays. Colleges that even mention us, say in their hygiene courses—they don't have to be supportive. If I taught a class and said, discreetly, that homosexuals exist—wham, no funding. I hope they'll defeat it, but who knows? We're not so far from the Dark Ages."

"With this third-rate actor in the White House, taking food from the poor, and the CIA killing poor farmers in Nicaragua, and all. But Erika, things do get better. You remember what a time we had buying a house together—now there's a protective ordinance. Remember when Hannah's husband took her kids away from her? Now we're winning custody suits—sometimes."

Erika smiled. "I must say I like our house. It beats the Honeymoon Hotel, doesn't it?"

Frances stood up and began stacking the dishes. "Don't put down the Honeymoon Hotel. We were happy there, remember?"

TWO

It was late-morning hot. Sunshine glimmered through the rips in the window shade and lay in streaks across the floor. Frances' head ached, her neck was stiff, and she felt sweaty and sticky. She opened her eyes cautiously. The room came into focus: spots on the oatmeal-colored wallpaper, crumpled sheet, and flimsy pink rayon bedspread, and on the floor a stack of newspapers and a little pile of discarded clothes. Across the room was an old-fashioned dresser with a swinging mirror and a little heap of objects visible but not identifiable in the sun's glare.

Erika lay on her back, delicate ribs showing through sweat-damp skin, the birdlike bones of her outflung arms asking for compassion. Such a strong woman, Frances thought, strong enough for both of us, and she looks so frail. She wanted to take Erika in her arms and cradle her against some unspecified danger.

As though the thought had awakened her, Erika moved and sighed, then opened her eyes and smiled. "I thought maybe I was dreaming you."

"I'm real, all right."

"How is your face?"

Frances felt her cheek with careful fingers, the crusting scab where Bill's fist had broken the skin. "It's going to be all right. It isn't feverish or anything. Are you sorry you took me in?"

"No, how could I be? Are you?

"Happy, but my head aches." Hadn't they promised to be truthful with each other, to say what they thought? She said quickly, "I'll be all right as soon as I get some coffee. What are we going to do today?"

6

"Nothing. *Ganz nichts.* It's Sunday, a nice day with sunshine. Tomorrow we go to the employment office with our most serious faces on, and see who has the privilege of hiring us. When we have a couple of paychecks, we can find a better place to live."

"You make it sound so easy."

"It can't be too difficult. Millions of people are doing it all the time, and some of them are quite stupid. We are not stupid."

"I don't know how to do anything. I'm a dumb housewife."

"Of course you do. Switchboard and receptionist. Checkout clerk in a grocery store. Cashier in a drugstore. Waiting on tables. No, that is too hard on the feet. You could do housework if you had to, what else have you been doing for the last twenty years?" She looked at Frances' dismayed face, and laughed. "That seems degrading to you, that's low-class? I'd rather sweep and wash dishes for someone else than for myself, it's the same work and they pay you for it."

Frances sat up and hung her legs over the side of the bed, silently but firmly rejecting housework.

"I tell you what we'll do after we have breakfast, we'll go to see Vince. He might know someone who needs you. You could sell things in a store."

"Vince has done so much for us already."

"He likes that, to help his friends. Haven't you noticed? But not before noon, because he might have brought someone home from the bar."

Frances considered this. It was her first glimpse of the network that exists for any oppressed minority, a network that would supply job references, court testimony, medical care, telephone numbers, sympathy; and even, in extremity, cash. She had supposed that Vince was helping Erika and her because he liked them. All right, he did like them, but he would have helped them anyway. She had joined, without knowing it, a secret society. Vince was her brother in the submerged world of Gay.

For Erika there was no conflict. If you loved, you were committed. They needed jobs. All right, they would find jobs,

maybe not the ones they wanted but useful in that they would
pay for rent and food. If the work was unpleasaⅬt, if the em-
ployers were uncongenial, they would hang on while they looked
for something better. Life was like that. If the pay was too low,
if it took an hour to get to work by bus, there were always other
possibilities. At the very worst they could go on welfare — but
Erika had never been on welfare. She didn't look down on people who were, but for herself she would protect her privacy
by working as long as she could. Income assured, they would
throw their few belongings into a friend's car and set up a household, washing floors, spraying for roaches, painting furniture
from the Catholic Salvage and the Salvation Army.

There were minor discomforts. She had lived through Steinhagen, she had the purple tattoo on her arm to remind her of
it. She was a survivor.

Erika said, smiling, "Welcome to Honeymoon Hotel, the
romantic resort."

"I wish we were out in the country under a tree."

"I promise we'll have a tree someday." Erika reached out,
the numbers on her arm showing dark in the morning sunlight.
"This isn't bad. We have a key, and no one can come in unless
we say so."

Frances thought a little resentfully: any time I start feeling
sorry for myself, she can hit me with some kind of moral
superiority. She said, "I grew up cold and hungry, I was a coal
miner's child, there's nothing romantic about growing up in a
coal town . . ."

"It's a long time since you were hungry, or took a bath in
a washtub."

"Sure. And I lived in a country where there was plenty of
everything, if you could only get hold of it. And I was a member of the master race." She was following Erika's thoughts.
"Only there were a lot of people who never figured out how
to get their share of the good things, and my folks were some
of them. I suppose that was part of Bill's appeal to me, he'd
always had everything, he looked like security. Of course that
didn't work out so well."

"There are Bills in the coal towns, too."

An old anger was rising in Frances; she didn't want to feel it today, her first day with Erika. She had left Bill — she felt the lump on her cheek — and there was nothing left of him except — "Erika, my engagement ring! It must be worth several hundred dollars."

"Vince has a friend who has a jewelry store. We can ask him to assess it. It's good to have something we can fall back on if we are sick."

That made sense. The Kirbys never had a bank account, never had anything they could sell or pawn in an emergency. And Bill Ollenfield's money was his. He was open-handed with it (give the devil his due), he went over the charge accounts every month and okayed what she had bought, but of course she only bought what he wanted her to have. What she wanted had nothing to do with it. Frances felt better. This was a new world, she felt awkward and ignorant in it, but she hadn't come to Erika empty-handed. Having snatched the ring from her dressing table drawer on impulse while she was throwing things into her suitcase, she now saw that it was the best thing she could have done.

She said, "I suppose we ought to get up. I wonder what time it is."

"Almost noon, from the sun. The Brenners will be at their son's house for Sunday dinner, the Callahans go to eleven-o'clock mass. The bathroom is all ours." Erika stretched luxuriously. "Let's have breakfast, or brunch or something, and go to the park."

"Do we have anything to eat?"

"We'll go to the Y cafeteria. The food is quite good and there's no tipping. Tomorrow, after the employment agency, we can buy food."

The bathroom was warm, steamy, and highly scented with Mrs. Callahan's bargain bath salts, which smelled like cheap candy. Someone had cleaned the bathtub. Erika turned on both taps. "It's good to be clean. Doesn't last long in this weather."

"Beats a washtub." That memory was beginning to seem funny, now she had talked about it. She had always been silent and shamefaced when the Wives reminisced: summer camp, swimming lessons, boarding school, she had never had any of the things they took for granted. She had never seen a shower until she went to college, and then se was afraid to use it in front of the others; she crept into the bathroom in the middle of the night and experimented with all the little knobs until she knew how to work it. Giggling at the memory, she slid down into the warm water and took the washcloth Erika handed her. "I think we're going to be all right."

"Naturally. We're young and healthy, young enough anyway, and more intelligent than a lot of people. We can take care of ourselves. May I join you?"

"Please do."

"People get married without having any more money or learning than we have. At least we don't have to worry about getting pregnant."

Erika soaped the thin washcloth and attacked Frances' back. "I read once about a girl who had a lot of love affairs, just casual ones. She thought it was a terrible waste of time because she perspired, and then she had to take a bath. Finally she really fell in love and she said she understood what all those baths were about." She laughed. "There's a Yiddish saying, 'Venn man tantzt, man schwitzt.' Means you pay for your pleasures, I think."

"I like that kind of dancing."

Frances' mind flew back to Bill, a Bill smelling of whiskey and male sweat, sullenly determined to have his rights as a husband; a Bill who rolled over and fell asleep, leaving her to lie awake with her anger and frustration. She had tried to wash the memory of him out of her mind and off her body. Now all that was over. She was starting out new, with a woman who knew how she felt and loved her as she was.

But there was no way to wipe out the past. Bake was part of it — Bake, who had brought her out and then betrayed her, Bake who had beaten her up so that she came to her son's wedding with a black eye and puffy lip. And Bill, and Bob who had been a sweet little boy — but he wasn't a little boy anymore, he was married now and she would probably never see him again. Mari would always keep a firm grip on him. She pushed away the thought of the past. You had to live for now.

She came back into the present as Erika's hands reached across her shoulders and closed around her soap-slippery breasts; as Erika swivelled around in the tub to make slow, easy love to her. Little waves sloshed around them. Their knees and shoulders bumped the sides of the tub. "Sneak preview," Erika said. "Let's go and eat."

Quiet in clean shorts and shirts, wet hair neatly combed back, they walked down the front steps into the full blast of a summer noonday. Hardly any cars on the street, no shopping housewives; Sunday quiet. The YWCA cafeteria was about six blocks away, on the edge of the downtown district. Clean and plain, a place where people on Social Security could get a good meal at a reasonable price, today it held three or four pairs of aging women dressed for church, enjoying a late breakfast, and some family groups having an early lunch. A high-chair baby chewed happily on a chicken bone. Already several items were crossed off the blackboard; the chicken was gone and so were the veal chops. "You can eat the meatloaf here," Erika said, accepting her plate over the counter. They paid, found a table near the window, and settled down to their meal. Frances said dreamily, "When we find a place with a stove, I'll make you a meatloaf. I'm a good cook."

"Me too. Martha taught me when I lived with her. But when I'm alone, I mostly eat yogurt and peanut butter."

Frances had never heard of Martha Weber before.

"She was my English teacher when I first came to this country. I lived with her for a while. She took me away from the first place where I lived, because things were going badly for me there." Erika was silent for a moment, looking back into a past she seldom thought about. "I won't lie to you, she was my lover for a while, the last year we lived together. She was like a mother and a lover all in one person."

"Did she bring you out?"

"No, the girl where I was staying did, but she was a bad person. She was like your Bake, I think. Lesbians are not always angels."

Frances said dryly, "I've noticed."

There seemed nothing more to say on that subject. They emptied their plates, had more iced tea, and walked out into the sunny afternoon with a fine feeling of leisure. Erika said, "We could take a bus to the park."

"I didn't know there was a park."

"Your husband and his friends wouldn't think much of it, but it's a wonderful place for poor people. They take their lunch and stay all day. There are trees."

In fact, it was a small and shabby park, set aside by the city a long time before and almost forgotten except for a single caretaker who fed the animals and tried to keep the weeds down. There was a shallow lagoon and plenty of trees, as Erika had promised; under their shade, families and young couples lay on blankets relaxing after the week's work or the week's search for work. Frances had seen Waubonsie as a typical midwestern town populated mostly by whites, but many of these people were black or hispanic. Young people wearing as little as the law allowed lay together and dozed, perhaps a little closer than the law approved. Boys played ball in a dusty hollow, the bases marked by stones. Little children waited for their turns on the two swings and the teeter-totter. A young man drowsed with his arm across a sleeping baby. An old man sat on a green bench reading the Sunday paper.

Frances said, "It's like a big back yard."

"It's the only yard some people have. Including us."

"What would happen if we'd lie on a blanket and hold hands?"

"Hard to tell. Let's look at the animals."

The bear was asleep, looking hot and frowzy, and the monkey sat in his tree and ignored them, but three raccoons came out of their house and held out their little black hands for peanuts. The smallest caught Frances' finger and held on like a baby. Dusty sparrows hopped around, looking for food. Frances said again, "I wish we could lie under a tree."

"You really like trees, don't you? Someday we'll have one. For now we have to get along with the good old Honeymoon Hotel."

It was something. Not enough, but something. They would have privacy, and a bed to make love on, and if they had to lie sometimes, because of a world that didn't acknowledge their kind of love, that was a small thing and they didn't need to feel guilty about it. They could go into a room and lock the door, and the room would be their home because they were in it together. The house on Commonwealth Avenue had never been home to Frances; it belonged to Bill.

They sat on a bench for a while and listened to a hungry-looking boy play a recorder. At the exit they stopped at a little wooden shack and bought ice cream cones from a fat woman who looked as if her feet hurt. The homeward bus was full of people going back to wherever they lived, looking relaxed. You can live well on just a little money, Frances told herself. These women in cheap shorts and discount store sandals managed to enjoy their lives. Some of them probably worked in Bill's factory; their work had paid for her custom-made drapes and Oriental rug.

She said, "We forgot factory work."

"The assembly line? If you have quick fingers and don't mind being bored all day."

Frances said, "I'm forty-one-years-old and I've never earned my own living."

"Oh well, I'm thirty-three and I worked all my life. What do I have to show for it? We'll get by—I keep telling you."

"We won't get pregnant. If we do, we'll probably have group insurance."

They smothered their laughter, sliding past closed stores and almost-empty downtown sidewalks. Frances was still thinking about the people she had seen, thinking about the people shut into solitary rooms, alone and bored. She said, "I like the park. People seem sort of together there."

They climbed the wooden steps of the Honeymoon Hotel and went into the cool dust-smelling downstairs hall and looked through the mail on the hall table, from habit and not because they expected anything. Erika said, shutting the bedroom door behind them, "Alone at last."

They fell into each other's arms like two eighteen-year-olds who had spent the afternoon on a blanket under a tree.

THREE

The sun wasn't quite so bright on Monday morning. They heated water for instant coffee on the hot plate, dressed carefully, and went out into the humid day without saying much, hardly looking at each other. The streets were full of people on their way to work, people with a place to go and a paycheck coming on the fifteenth.

Frances thought, "A week ago I was Mrs. William Ollenfield, with a big house and a pocketbook full of charge cards. Security, they call it. But the only security is what you make for yourself. I'll trade Bill Ollenfield for a job any day. A job doesn't come home drunk. A job doesn't invade your body in the middle of the night and leave you wishing it would go away. Only —"

She glanced at Erika, who was walking too fast and looking calm and serious, as she always did when she was worried. Neat in skirt and blouse, her hair pulled back, a pair of tiny gold rings in her ears, she looked like a college girl. Frances felt untidy and uncertain beside her, the bruise on her cheek covered with pancake makeup and her eyes heavy. She would need glasses soon — well, forty, what do you expect?

At half-past nine in the morning there were about thirty people in the waiting room of the Illinois State Employment Service. Mostly women. Mostly young, doing a bit of coughing and foot-shuffling while they waited, whispering to their girl friends. Not one had a book or a piece of knitting to pass the time. Up front, behind a little fence, two bored-looking young women were going through stacks of paper. A young black man, rather excessively well dressed, beckoned to a woman in the front row. Let me not have to talk to him, Frances thought, and was ashamed of herself. Still, he did look as though he might be overcompensating for whatever prejudice had been directed at him.

She did have to talk to him, as it turned out. He looked at the card she had filled out. "You forgot your Social Security number."

"I don't have one."

His eyebrows went up. "Don't have a Social Security number?"

"I've always kept house."

"You'll have to get one. Can't work without it." He wasn't unkind, it was just that he looked unutterably bored.

She said, "I'm quick to learn."

"One year of college, right?"

Well, not quite. She had left before the end of her freshman year to marry that goodlooking Bill Ollenfield, the only man who had ever given her a second look. But Mr. Patterson wouldn't be interested in that. He spent thirty-seven-and-a-half hours a week interviewing people who wanted to appear in the best possible light, people he would never see again.

"How would you feel about working as salad chef in a cafeteria? It's only five hours a day and the pay is low, but you'd get a good lunch. They want someone neat and clean, who speaks English without an accent." Like a side of beef, she thought, U.S. Government Inspected. "Ten-thirty to three-thirty, six days a week. That come out, let's see, at two-fifty that comes out around seventy-five a week, take-home sixty, unless you have dependents."

She said, "No dependents," but he wasn't listening. He picked up the phone, dialed a number and spoke quickly in a low monotone. They all did that, so you couldn't hear what they were saying. "They'll interview you. Take the C bus right across the street. Here's your appointment slip. If you get it, you better stop in at the Social Security office and apply for a card, because they'll start deducting right away. Call in and let me know."

"I will. Thank you."

He looked surprised. Weren't you supposed to thank people?

She hoped Erika would see her leave, but Erika was talking to one of the other officers and made no sign.

Suppose they don't like me? I'll go back and try again. Suppose the bus driver doesn't tell me where to get off? Okay, I'll walk back. Stop being silly, there are lots of jobs. Not for women over forty—the magazines say so, the TV programs. I have to get this job.

She got it.

Mrs. Cowan, sixty if she was a day, with gorgeous henna hair and bunion oxfords, took to her on sight. "I'll give you a week's try. If you don't like us or we don't like you, no hard feelings. Now you'll need a uniform. You pay for your own uniform, and I want it neat and clean at all times. Get it at the little store on the corner, he'll give you a discount. Comfortable shoes, this job is murder on the feet."

"Thank you."

A flash of humor. "Don't thank me till you try it. You may be damning me by the end of the week."

The green uniform of the Bee Hive Cafeteria, with checked collar and pockets, was on display in the window of the store; either the Bee Hive changed employees often or other places used the same style. The owner, Mrs. Cowan's male contemporary, let her try it on in a little back room. "Dollar down, dollar a week. You keep the job you'll need another, have a change. I eat at the Bee Hive all the time, I'll be seeing you. You a widow?"

She didn't know whether he was a prospecting widower or if he was just being friendly. If she was a widow she had better be a recent and heartbroken one. She sighed and nodded.

Social Security. The office was a cubbyhole in a municipal building, less dingy than the employment office. She filled out a card: Frances Ann Kirby, birthdate and place, mother's maiden name, marital status—divorced. Just anticipating the truth. She felt as if she had been given back to herself, as if all the years between the young Frances Kirby who set off t college with a borrowed suitcase, and this middle-aged salad chef had disappeared.

She didn't know how to get back to the Honeymoon Hotel from where she was. She took another C bus downtown and walked all the way back before she realized that she couldn't get in. Erika was not yet home. By this time it was well past noon. She was hungry. She urgently needed a bathroom; after thinking it over she rang the landlady's bell and asked if she might use the john, was led through an overstuffed living room and interrogated. "You going to stay here long? It's sixteen a week for double occupancy."

"Just a couple days." God, now what have I done? She didn't know how much rent Erika was paying, but of course it would be more for two. She went back out and sat on the porch, too worried to be hungry any more.

Erika plodded up the walk as if her feet hurt. "Hi. How long have you been waiting?"

"Not very long."

Erika sat down on the top step and took off her loafers and nylons. "Let's go down to Kenny's and have a sandwich. Unless you already ate."

"I got the job."

"I went two places and got 'we'll let you know.' "

Kenny greeted them like old friends. "Draw two in the dark, right? How's your face? You want a piece of custard pie?"

"Maybe later. I want a Denver sandwich."

Frances felt her cheek. "Healing up. Kenny, I just got a job."

"Hey, that's great! The pie is on me, to celebrate."

Erika said, "I don't think I was meant to be a switchboard operator or package wrapper." She took her shoes off again. "Will the Board of Health care?"

"Those bozos don't eat here." He refilled their cups and devoted himself to the grill.

"Erika, what would you do for a living if you had your choice?"

"Go back to teaching. I really liked that. Only after Kate — I didn't feel like working for a while."

"Could you get a job?"

"Oh sure, there are always last-minute vacancies. Somebody gets pregnant, or her husband gets transferred. I'd have
to register my certificate, take some refresher courses."

"How much would it cost?"

"Two hundred, maybe. I haven't got it."

"We have the ring."

"That's for emergencies."

"What do you call this?"

"Well, yes, if it was my ring I'd do it in a flash."

"It's ours."

"Bill Ollenfield would love that."

"To hell with him, I earned it. Besides, we're going to be
paying more rent. Your landlady cornered me and asked how
long I'm staying. I get the feeling she doesn't approve of my
being there."

"Snoopy old bitch. We'll move at the end of the week, when
the rent runs out. Though it would take her a month to evict
us if she wanted to get technical about it."

"Maybe we can find a place with a kitchen. I like to cook."

"I never expected to be in love with a salad chef." Erika
kissed her. Either Kenny wasn't looking or he didn't care.

Frances felt pleased and proud. She was going to get Erika
back into her own line of work. She had a job; she could do
her share. "Kenny, how are the sandwiches doing? I'm starved."

It was three in the afternoon. Thirty-eight hours ago she
and Erika had been sitting at this same counter, reassuring themselves about the future. Now they were being pushed into it
headfirst.

She should have been scared, but she wasn't. She felt great.

FOUR

"I've never been so tired in my life."

"It's a poor time for it." Erika wiped her sweaty face on her sleeve. "There's no rest till we get the bed made, at least. It's a good thing we don't own much stuff."

"It's a good thing Vince bought a car, much as I hate to think of him turned loose in traffic." Vince's car was fourth-hand, and he drove with more confidence than skill. So far he hadn't broken down in the rush-hour traffic. Perhaps they wouldn't, either.

Erika said, "It's surprising how things multiply when you move. I never owned anything but a sleeping mat and rice bowl, and now all this."

"Time's moving so fast it makes me dizzy. Like being on a merry-go-round that won't stop."

"Really dizzy?"

Frances stopped to consider. "No, figuratively."

Erika looked relieved. "Next time we move, we'll hire someone. By that time we can afford it."

Frances shoved the last box into the back of the car. "If we hit a bump we're out of luck, they way the springs are sagging."

"What springs?" Erika climbed into the driver's seat. "Look, no more stairs, a separate entrance, a nice little kitchen, and the landlord's a brother. He won't care if we make love all day and all night."

"I will. We'd be too tired to work. And little is the word for the kitchen. If I bend over to look in the oven, my behind sticks out into the bedroom. But it's nice to have an oven," she added hastily, afraid Erika would think she was complaining. "I'll bake you a cake for Sunday dinner."

"This Sunday or next?"

"One week from today."

Erika started the car, rather jerkily. "What are you going to do about your winter clothes?" she asked when they were finally in the southbound lane.

"It's ninety in the shade."

"Be winter before you know it. You ought to call him—" Erika avoided saying his name, she preferred to think of him as an abstraction, or better, not at all. "Make some arrangement to pick up what belongs to you. Your clothes are no use to him."

"I never want to see him again."

"He'll have to be served with papers when you get your divorce. Your address will be on them, I suppose. Whether he shows up in court or not. You won't get any alimony—I know, you don't want it and you're right—but you have a right to your personal things. Winter coats cost money."

Frances didn't want to think about the divorce. She had been in a courtroom only once, after the disastrous breakup with Bake, and the memory was a sore spot in her mind. And she certainly didn't want to see Bill, or talk to him. Vince had asked, "What can he do to you?" "Nothing. I just don't want to see him."

They were using Vince's lawyer as well as his car. All she knew about Sherman Kolb was that he was young, prematurely bald, had a front marriage, and would let her pay thirty dollars a month for ten months. Anyone could get a divorce. All she had to do was show up in the courtroom, preferably in a skirt, and say Yes and No. He would ask about the cut face—too bad there wasn't a scar, Kolb said. You didn't have to be Clarence Darrow to get a divorce in Illinois, it was all in a day's work.

She still didn't want to think about it.

She said, "You're the one who has a right to be tired."

For Erika was going to school in the morning, clerking in the dime store in the afternoon and working as cashier in a snack shop three evenings a week, coming home at two in the morning.

Erika said matter-of-factly, "I am tired. I just don't see any point in making a fuss about it. It won't last forever." She took one hand off the steering wheel to pat Frances on the shoulder. "This is the hardest time, right now."

Vince was waiting at the new place, either from a desire to be helpful or because he didn't quite trust them with his car. He had never owned a car before and was unreasonably proud of it, considering the shape it was in. He grabbed the box of dishes and started up the walk with it. "Nice set of match luggage you got here."

"All from the same liquor store."

They stood looking at each other in the small bedroom. "Why do places always look so little when they're empty" "Because there's nothing to compare them with. It's *Gestalt*." Vince found a stick and propped open the window with it. "I'll get some sash cords, they're not hard to put in. Nice view." It was the brick wall of the building next door.

Erika said, "Anyway, no one can see in. I've had trouble with people peeking under the venetian blinds, where I lived before."

Frances sat down on the floor and closed her eyes. Vince said, "If you will make mad love all night."

Erika asked, "Who has time to make love? I got in at three and she didn't even turn over. The bars close at one and Mary's place is open till two—every old lush in Waubonsie comes in to sober up on black coffee. They all want to walk me home —I never had so many propositions in my life—"

"Tell them you have a big, jealous husband waiting up for you."

"So now Mary sends me home in a taxi. She's all right."

"Phil worked there once, and she bailed him out when he got caught in a bath raid."

Frances sat looking blankly at the cardboard boxes that held their belongings. Gin, Vermouth, Rum, Johnny Walker Black Label. Vince suggested, "Let's go out and eat. You can unpack later."

Frances ignored him. "I shouldn't have complained. I was upset about my check. Forty-two dollars and eighty cents. Who gave the government any right to take all that money out of my pay? I worked for that money. It's almost a fourth of what I make. They take it out without asking me and they don't pay any interest on it."

"You'll get Social Security when you're old."

"I need it right now."

Vince said soothingly, "That's the system. How's the job otherwise?"

Frances considered. "All right, I guess. They call me a chef, but it's just housework, like getting ready for the bridge club, only more so. It would be easier if you could stop making salads and sweep the floor or make the beds or something—not so monotonous. I can hardly stand to eat lettuce any more."

"I've missed you at the store. You'd don't have to buy anything, you could just drop in on your way to work."

"We'll be in as soon as we get settled." Frances put a hand on Vince's shoulder and got up from the floor. "I hope you know how much we appreciate all this. We'll pay you back somehow."

"Just stay as sweet as you are. Shall we eat? The Y won't care how you look. They'll think we're a hippie commune."

"They'll think we're moving."

"I should have put on my gold eyelashes. A touch of class, a touch of éclat. Speaking of éclat, I could eat one, a big gooey one with chocolate frosting."

"You fool."

"I love you, too."

They walked to the Y. Erika said it was faster than driving and besides, where would they park? Frances said it was an extravagance. "We ate here last week."

"When my ship comes in I'll take you to the Golden Peacock," Vince offered.

"God forbid." The Golden Peacock, long on liquor and decor, was where Bill's crowd went to celebrate promotions and anniversaries. "We'll cook you a good dinner as soon as we're settled."

Vince set his tray on a corner table and sank into a chair. "You know, you two really have it made. It may not feel that way right now. You're tired, everything's happening too fast, you're having a hard time paying the bills." Frances glared at him. She didn't need to be reminded how tired she was, but he smiled sweetly. "The worst is over and you're on your way. As soon as Erika's qualified to teach again, things will look better. Besides, you're worried about the divorce."

"I don't even want to think about it."

She ached all over. There was a slice of ham and a sweet potato on the plate in front of her, but she was too tired to pick up the fork. Her feet were too big for her shoes, her hair was stringy and her arms ached. How could Erika love such a mess? She looked at Erika, who had developed some eye-corner wrinkles overnight. maybe we're too old to start over, maybe it's too much effort.

All she could think of, to cheer herself up, was that anything was better than being married to Bill Ollenfield and playing canasta with the Wives. Even if she and Erika never had enough energy to make love again—and at this moment it seemed distinctly possible—they were together for better, for worse, till life us do part. It might not look like much in their state of spaced-out tiredness, but it was what they had.

FIVE

The courtroom was the drabbest place Frances had ever seen. She didn't know what she had expected—certainly not pageantry and pomp and the majesty of the law, certainly not the melodrama of a TV story. Here in Waubonsie the same building housed federal, state, and municipal courts. The walls were the same dingy green as those of the employment office, and the wooden enclosure around the jury box seemed trivial. The American flag and the state flag flanking the judge's dais were grimy. The judge, appearing through a side door in a business suit and lopsided tie, was shifty-eyed and in need of a haircut. It was frightening. This place held such power—for some people, power over life and death—and it looked so unimportant.

There were only a dozen people in the room, and Bill was not among them. Sherman Kolb sat alone at the end of a pew —they did look like pews—looking as though he had just dropped in to pay the light bill or pick up a loaf of bread. She considered joining him, but thought there might be a rule against it. She slipped into the back row and sat down, then realized that the others were rising and got to her feet.

Erika had offered, not very convincingly, to call in sick and come with her. This was the second week of September, the beginning of a new semester at the community college. "Don't be silly. You can't afford to miss your class." Now she wished she had someone there for moral support—almost anyone.

She sat down so hard that the wooden bench hurt the backs of her knees. If I have to wait very long, she thought, I'll probably faint and have to be carried out. Or drop dead. Or die of thirst—her throat ached with dryness, she couldn't have said a word to save her life. Two men were standing in front of the judge, one talking in a low voice, the other looking stubborn. She wished she could hear what was being said.

Sherman Kolb turned and nodded at her as the two men retreated. She nodded back, and then realized that he was waiting for her to walk down that endless aisle and stand in front of the judge. She made it without stumbling. Sherman winked at her. Nice, she thought, he does this all the time, nice of him to understand that I'm nervous. Nervous? Half dead with fright.

Someone held a Bible out to her, gabbled through the oath — she had seen this on TV a hundred times — and Sherman asked her a few questions. The whole truth? Well, she had been a good and faithful wife, at least she hadn't been involved with other men (never mind Bake). Yes, Bill struck her, endangering her life and health. No, she had no support from him after she left. No, she didn't want alimony. She answered Sherman, knowing that the real facts of her marriage and separation would never be told, wondering if it was like that for all the good, inarticulate people who appeared here. What went on the record might be the literal truth, but it wasn't the real truth.

Not only had Bill not turned up, he hadn't bothered to hire a lawyer. The suit was uncontested. Glad to get rid of her, probably. She was thinking about this when Sherman Kolb took her by the elbow and led her past all the almost-empty benches and out into the hall. "I'll mail you the decree. You understand that you can resume your maiden name? You'll have to change it with any stores where you have charge accounts, and the IRS and Social Security. Oh yes, and the utility companies. You may find it harder to open charge accounts now you're single." She choked down a desire to tell him that she and Erika lived on a cash-and-carry basis. Erika said their credit rating was so bad, the stores would hardly let them pay cash. The thought of filling out income tax forms worried her — Bill's company lawyer had always done his — but Erika said not to worry until they had more income. Anyway Vince would know somebody.

Dear Vince, a faithful friend since the day she wandered into his secondhand store and first met Erika.

"Good luck, kid. Let me know if you run into any problems." Transformed from a lawyer into a friend, he gave her a peck on the cheek and got into his small sporty car, leaving her with the rest of the day and a feeling of emptiness, as if a load had been lifted from her chest.

Free, she thought. I'll never have to see Bill again. Of course I'll never see Bob either, but he doesn't need me, he has Mari and he is his father's son, he wouldn't want to see me anyhow. Free to live with Erika and be as happy as life will let us be.

It was almost noon. Mrs. Cowan had given her the day off; twice divorced herself, she would want to hear all the details, but Frances didn't feel like seeing Mrs. Cowan or washing lettuce. Besides, she had on her only dress; she had brought nothing but slacks and shorts from the big walk-in closet on Commonwealth Avenue. She walked slowly to the edge of the shopping area and found herself in front of Vince's place, half antique shop and half junk. A Tiffany-style lamp, an old plush photograph album and a campy orange feather duster shared the show window. Poor picking, business was bad. She went in. Vince was sitting on the counter reading, in the absence of customers. "Well, how did it go?"

"Just like you said, short and sweet. Sherman put it through without a hitch."

"You don't look too happy."

"Tired. It hasn't got to me yet."

"You chicks going out to celebrate?"

"I haven't thought about it. Erika's pretty busy with classes and two jobs."

"Come on, it's an occasion. The Happi Time is having an anniversary party—I'll take you for half an hour and buy you one drink, you ought to be able to stand that. You ever see a drag show?"

She shook her head. "I thought the Happi Time was a men's bar."

"Mixed, for something like this. You wanna go? You don't have to stay if you're bored."

"It's up to Erika." That seemed safe; she couldn't see Erika at a drag show.

But Erika, coming through the door with an armful of workbooks as they sat drinking coffee and eating crackers and cheese, looked surprised and then amused. "Sure, why not? Fran never

saw a drag show. Beautiful women, only they're not. Gorgeous
evening dresses, and sometimes there's music. If we don't stay
long, if we just have one drink." She didn't ask about the hearing, and Frances found that she was relieved. It was already
beginning to seem like part of the past. But then, Frances reminded herself, so many bad things have happened in Erika's
life that she doesn't worry any more.

While Vince carried the cups into the kitchen, she found
a moment to say, "It's okay. He didn't show. Didn't care, I guess."

"That's good."

"I suppose." But she felt a little slighted.

The bar they went to was in the heart of downtown, not
more than three blocks from Woolworth's. Frances supposed
she had walked past it a dozen times without ever knowing it
was there. No neon; there was a small sign in script on the
door. They climbed the front steps, spoke to a man at the door,
and paid two dollars apiece. And were in a fairyland of light
and color, lights slowly revolving over a fabric-draped wall.
Fifty or sixty young men and a dozen older ones sat chatting,
greeting newcomers. Three women at the bar gave Frances and
Erika a cool look as they found seats. Or were they women?
Yes, dykes—that appraising look could be a lead-in to cruising.

Rows of folding chairs faced the stage, and as Vince brought
drinks—one martini each, Erika specified—the lights dimmed
and a dapper emcee in white tie and tails walked out from
behind the purple curtain. They had arrived just in time for the
show.

Frances had seen fashion shows. Department stores were
always putting them on, and the Wives loved them, would go
to any luncheon that was a framework for mannequins showing off expensive new clothes. She took the smallest possible
sip of her drink as the curtain went up to show a runway banked
with artificial flowers. A string trio at the back of the room
drifted into a soft sentimental melody. The first model
—could this be a man?—appeared. Willowy and graceful, with
a definite cleavage above the gold lamé evening dress, he swayed
down the runway to music and applause. She looked inquir-

ingly at Vince, but he was leaning forward, absorbed in looking.

She was impressed. The setting was so well constructed,
the music so alluring — all right, Erika laughed at her taste in
music, but she like sentimental tunes, the *Blue Danube* could
make her cry — and the models were any teenage girl's notion
of glamour and sex appeal. It was impossible to believe that
these were men. Feather fans waved, five-inch heels on glittery
pumps sparkled and turned. The shows she had gone to with
the Wives were designed to sell clothes. Here the merchandise,
if there was any, was human. The luxurious showing-off of
women in the old-time brothels deluxe must have been like
this, she thought. It was a blur, a dazzle; the models came and
went so quickly that she couldn't get a clear impression of any
of them, yet she understood from what Vince had said on the
way over that this was a contest and the "women" would be
judged on appearance, taste, and popularity.

But why did men want to masquerade as women? She could
understand the need of some lesbians to imitate men, because
men had all the power. There were butches who wore jockey
shorts under their fly-front jeans and stomped around like truck
drivers in the movies (real truck drivers, she had noticed, looked
like anyone else). She sat back to enjoy the pageant for what it
was worth.

Erika's hand touched hers, lightly. "Can we go? I'm a little
tired."

They slipped out with a nod to Vince, who smiled absent-
mindedly and went on watching the show. He would be there
until they locked the doors.

Standing on the curb, watching for a cruising taxi, Erika
yawned. "It's pretty, isn't it? Like a Hollywood movie, like a
child's book of fairy tales. If life could only be like that — "

"It's like orchids. I don't like orchids much."

"No. I'll take dandelions."

Frances supposed their life would look like dandelions to
the glamorous creatures those dressed-up men were supposed
to represent. What had happened to the myth of the exotic,
glamorous lesbian practicing strange perversions? Did teenage

girls dream of her any more? What did they think when they finally got into bed with a woman and found her, exciting certainly, but real?

Never mind. She had what she wanted, and if there was a lot of salad-making involved that was all right too. Erika probably didn't find much artistic satisfaction in teaching long division to fourth-graders, either. You had to wash dishes, you had to take the sheets to the laundromat. If Vince got something out of watching imitation women slink around in evening dress, more power to him.

Stepping into the Yellow, she felt a homesick pang for her little apartment with the too-small kitchen and makeshift curtains. It was the first real home she had ever had. Not the company house in the shadow of the mine tipples, not the houses she had lived in with Bill Ollenfield, not even the Honeymoon Hotel, had been her own. Now she was married and she had a home. Put like that it sounded a little bit silly, hers was a subculture that had turned away from marriage, but she understood for the first time why some lesbian couples wore rings and observed anniversaries. For better or worse, she thought, holding Erika's hand.

SIX

"My God, it's cold! What time is it?"

"Just seven." Erika's voice was muffled. Her face emerged from the folds of her old brown sweater. "Heat's beginning to come up. Greg says the thermostat is set for seventy."

"The radiators were ice-cold at half past ten. They're supposed to keep it up to a certain level at night, I forget what." They had fallen into bed at eleven with their winter coats piled on top of the blankets.

"It's the chill factor. You can sleep another hour."

"No I can't, not without you to warm me up. Why did we rent this place anyhow?"

"Because it was summer," Erika said reasonably. "I've got the oven going and a pot of water boiling." She ran a comb through her hair, longer now in deference to the teaching profession but still hanging straight around her face. A pixie face, Frances thought, high cheekbones, sharp chin, wide eyes that were sometimes gray and sometimes green. She said, "You need a new coat."

"Next year. I'm glad you have your warm one." Vince had gone in a taxi to Bill Ollenfield's house, taking along a friend for moral support, and a note from Sherman Kolb authorizing him to pick up Frances' personal belongings. France had been both grateful and angry. "You should have asked me first."

"You'd have said no."

"What did he say?"

"Never said a mumblin' word. He went through the closets and drawers and put all the stuff in boxes and pointed to the door. Might have been mute as far as I could tell. Tommy and I carried the stuff out, and that was it."

"I sort of wish you hadn't done it."

30

"To hell with false pride, darling. The stuff is yours. You kept house for the man, didn't you? And slept with him. Figure twenty bucks a trick, that's a lot of bread."

"Vince, really."

"What's this fur? Looks like rabbit."

"It's nutria, and don't ask me what that is. May be rabbit for all I know. I'm going to sell it."

"You might sell the two formals to a drag queen, but they're sort of ladylike."

"You're impossible."

But of course he wasn't. He was their good friend, and she was glad she had her tan coat with the fur collar and her fur-lined overshoes. Vince was the closest thing to a brother that she had, and she loved him even when she was furious with him.

Chicago was having, in this winter of 1961, the coldest weather in more than a hundred years. Waubonsie, forty miles to the southwest, was suffering too. Heavy snow fell all day and night, piled up faster than the municipal plows could move it; moved, it lay in drifts across side streets and driveways. Sidewalks were slippery with ice, and the wind howled off lake Michigan and cut through the heaviest clothes. There was a wreck on the El. Cars skidded off the roads, vagrant drunks were found frozen stiff in doorways, and the chill factor went down to forty below zero. Mrs. Cowan, who owned her house and paid her own coal bills, admitted that she kept the thermostat at eighty and supplemented the furnace with an electric heater in the bathroom. The women in the cafeteria wore sweaters over their uniforms, and the customers kept their coats on while they gulped hot coffee—refills on the house.

Now Frances forced herself out of bed, put on her slippers, and headed into the tiny kitchen. It was warmer there, with the oven door open. She spooned instant coffee into a cup and added boiling water, wrapped her hands around the cup for warmth while she waited for it to cool. Erika came in, gave her a goodbye kiss and said, "Take a cab."

"It's an hour wait. Everybody's taking cabs now."

"Wrap up, anyhow. Never mind how you look." Erika bit into a half-eaten slice of toast spread with peanut butter, shook her head and put it down again. Breakfast didn't interest her; she was only trying to stoke up against the chill. She shut the door behind her, but not before the icy draft from the hall got in.

It was too cold for bathing. Frances dabbled here and there with a soapy washcloth and got into the warmest clothes she owned — a tee shirt under the uniform and a wool sweater over it — and cursed the day Mrs. Cowan had transferred her to the breakfast shift. Knee socks, lined stadium boots, a wool scarf over her face. A good thing we don't have a thermometer, she thought. If I knew how cold it is, I'd never go out. Wind blew in under the foyer door, wind with frost flakes glittering in it. She stepped out, hunching her shoulders as she left the sheltering lee of the building.

There were two muffled people on the street. The man next door was trying to start his car, clouds of steam puffing around him.

Halfway to the corner it happened. A bare patch of ice, a sickening feeling in the pit of her stomach as she went down, and a snapping sound as her left leg doubled under her. She tried to get up, and couldn't. But I have to, she thought wildly. I'll freeze. She stood up and fell, her leg crumpled under her.

Oh, God, do something. She hadn't prayed since she was a small child, she knew there wasn't anyone there, but now she started begging for someone to come and rescue her, not let her freeze in sight of her own building. Oh God, I don't want to die now, not at forty-two. Please listen.

Two men came out of the corner building, one swinging a bunch of keys, and stopped to look. "Hey, what's the matter? Slip on the ice?"

"I think I've broken my leg."

"Well." He was silent, and she knew why. He was supposed to be on the way to work. He was probably late as it was. But a man can't let someone freeze to death practically on his doorstep. He walked carefully over to her and grabbed an arm. His friend, after a momentary hesitation, took the other arm. They half-dragged, half-carried her to the car at the curb, got her into the back seat. "I'll bet it hurts like hell," the first one said.

"I'm too cold to tell."

At the entrance to City Hospital's emergency wing a chilled-looking orderly bundled her into a wheelchair and pushed her up a ramp and into the building. The leg was hurting now, more than she supposed anything could hurt. The nurse in admissions, with a red sweater over her uniform, looked sympathetic as she filled out the forms. In x-ray they cut away her boot and pulled off the nylon stocking and wool sock. "I know it hurts. Try to stand it a little longer."

She was shaking, whether with cold or pain or terror she didn't know. The radiators were clanking but the room was cold. So was the room into which they trundled her. The second bed was empty. "Need some help getting undressed?"

"I think I'm going to throw up."

Someone brought her a basin, but nothing happened. The aide helped her out of her clothes and into a thin, split-back nightshirt. The aide's hands were icy. She said chattily, "I almost froze in bed last night. Moved the thermostat up to eighty-five and it still wasn't warm. Hold the leg as still as you can." She was cheerful; it wasn't her leg that was broken.

The woman who came to take her case history, filling out long forms, also wore a sweater—an orange one, like a little bonfire in the frigid air of the room. Frances tried to focus on it. A bonfire was nice, you could warm your hands at it.

She needed to go to the bathroom. She felt sick. She lay with her head on a slippery pillow, and after a long time, several years probably, a young man in a tan jacket came in and said that her leg was certainly broken and she should stay overnight and wait for the swelling to go down so they could cast it. "You'll be in a cast for six to eight weeks. Got any insurance?"

Mrs. William Ollenfield had been loaded with insurance. Blue Cross, Blue Shield, major medical. Her husband's secretary had filled out the papers. Frances Kirby, a salad chef, had sixteen dollars between her and payday. She shook her head. "I was on my way to work."

"Too bad it didn't happen at work. OSHA would have paid the bills."

"Sure, I should have slipped on a lettuce leaf."

What would happen when Erika got home and she wasn't there? As though her thoughts were audible, the young doctor asked, "Anybody you want to notify? Family, employer?" She gave him Vince's home number — there was no phone in the store — and he went away and left her staring at a blank television screen.

Someone brought her a bedpan and, some time later, carried it away again. Some else brought her a tray with soup and Jello, and a glass of water with, of all things, an ice cube in it. An aide showed her how to ring for the nurse and how to raise and lower the head of the bed. "Don't monkey with the foot, they've got your leg propped on a pillow." She grinned, "Be grateful they haven't put an ice pack on it."

The telephone on the bedside stand worked. She tried to think of someone to call, tried the Frances E. Willard Elementary School, where Erika was doing her practice teaching, and got a busy signal. She thought of calling Mrs. Cowan at work, but by this time the lunch rush would be on and anyway Vince would let her know.

She wished she had something to read.

And how do we ever pay for all this? In Chicago there would have been Cook County, dingy, overcrowded, but set up to provide free health care for the poor. Here everything had to be paid for, and she would have no income for six weeks — longer, because Mrs. Cowan certainly couldn't hold the job for her. Would Greg wait for the rent? I'm starting to sound like a soap opera, she told herself, but it isn't funny. If I ever get back on my feet, I'm going to look for a job with fringe benefits.

They had been realistic about money. Some lesbian couples put everything in a joint account, guaranteeing trouble when they broke up. Other split the household bills down the middle or prorated them, the partner with the larger income paying more. They hadn't really made any decisions. There wasn't

enough money coming in to allow for planning — poor people
don't budget, they manage. Frances and Erika paid the rent,
bought food, and were usually reduced to going through their
coat pockets for change the last few days before payday. The
restaurant paid every week, chinking in the cracks between
Erika's various checks. They didn't buy anything that wasn't
absolutely necessary.

Another doctor came in and looked at her foot. "They should
have put an ice pack on it."

"In this weather? Have a heart!"

"Okay, but you'll be sorry if the cast breaks, and it's going
to itch more, too, if it's too loose." A candy-striper brought her
a little package: toothbrush, massage lotion, tissues, and a blue
booklet entitled *Your Rights as a Patient.* She decided not to
read it. Another candy-striper brought a long mimeographed
menu and asked her to check her choices for supper. She could
have meatloaf or salmon patties, broccoli or string beans, a baked
apple or stewed prunes. What was this, a hotel? She said, "Just
bring me a pizza," but the candy-striper, every day of seventeen, took her work seriously and was not amused.

They brought in a patient for the other bed, an old lady
still groggy after surgery, who moaned and muttered. The nurse
looked around the dividing curtain to ask, "Are you in pain?"
"No, I'm cold," Frances told her. "I think all the extra blankets
are in use. Try and sleep." She tried, but it wasn't much use.
The hall was full of footsteps and voices and clanking noises.

She was asleep out of pure boredom when Erika arrived
at half-past four, red-faced and breathless with cold. "Good grief,
they're already pushing supper carts around. I bet they wake
you at five and make you brush your teeth before breakfast."

"I'm so sorry about this."

"Why? You didn't do it on purpose."

The other patient's husband came in, looking abashed and
carrying a bunch of carnations. He was a small, bald man who
looked a little like a rabbit. His wife moved and muttered something as he pulled the curtain shut behind him. There was no
sound from behind the curtain; Frances supposed the patient
was still asleep. The silence gave her a feeling of privacy.

Erika took off her scarf, knitted cap, coat, and sweater, and leaned to give Frances a polite kiss. "Does it hurt much?"

"Not as long as I lie still. They're going to put a cast on it tomorrow." She looked imploringly at Erika. "I don't know when I can go back to work, or if I'll even have a job.

"We'll manage." Erika had been managing since she was twelve. She was good at it.

Frances said, "You know, I never thought about it before, but I'd like to do something in a hospital. I don't mean like aides or Gray Ladies, I mean something professional. Not a nurse, I think. I know they do valuable work and the pay is pretty good, but they take orders and then the doctors get all the credit. I'd like to do x-ray or something."

"Not x-ray, it's too dangerous. Some kind of a technician or therapist. Other people learn — I don't think it takes too long."

"I'm sort of old."

"Older women are more responsible. They don't stay out all night and come in hung over. They don't get pregnant and quit, they don't have kids of their own to take care of. I read it in the *Ladies Home Journal*."

"I see you reading the *Ladies Home Journal*."

"In the dentist's office. You want the TV on? I happen to have a quarter."

"No, I have some change if I need it." Someone had brought in her purse and she put it under her pillow, just to have something familiar at hand. "My roommate will probably have it on. She looks like the kind who listens to all the soap operas."

"What's the matter with her?"

"I think she had some kind of surgery."

"They'll probably let you come home tomorrow."

"I sure hope so. How are we going to pay for all this?"

"The way we pay for everything — somehow. You take a taxi home."

"You take a taxi home. It's getting dark, and I don't suppose it's warmed up any. And you eat a good supper, you hear?"

"If you say so." Erika kissed her again, a real kiss this time. "I love you," she said softly.

"Likewise, I'm sure."

She was asleep before they brought the supper trays.

SEVEN

Winter went on forever. The Chicago papers said it was the coldest on record. The *Tribune* ran the temperature and chill factor in a box on the front page, and carried stories of flophouses full to overflowing and old people found frozen to death in their low-rent apartments. "That's news?" Erika asked. "In August they run a picture of a pretty girl frying eggs on the sidewalk." Frances said, "I only hope we live that long."

In Waubonsie the hospitals were full, the towing companies got rich, pipes froze and burst, and homeowners waited a month for a plumber. Stalled cars were abandoned by the roadsides. People who lived in the plush suburbs and worked downtown simply stayed home.

It was December, and the Salvation Army people stood on corners ringing their bells, steam rising from their pinched noses as they waited for people to drop coins in the kettle. It was too cold to think of singing. The stores managed an illusion of warmth and welcome with brightly decorated windows, but people did their buying and went home as early as they could. Erika, lighting the oven for warmth and dishing up the evening soup, said, "We'll survive."

She had borrowed money from the bank to pay Frances' hospital bill and the first term's tuition for a course in physical therapy. It would take three years to qualify. Phil, Greg's lover, bundled her into his car every morning and picked her up at noon, refusing payment for all the taxi service. Vince came to Sunday-night supper and handed her a hundred dollars — his entire savings, probably. "It's just layin' around." She burst into tears, which embarrassed him.

With a heavy wool sock over her cast, she hopped around from classroom to classroom and told Erika she was becoming a celebrity at school. "Not because of the leg, though they'd all like to practice on it, but I'm the same age as their mothers. Do you realize I'll be forty-five by the time I qualify?"

"Keep your mind off the hot flashes."

They cooked a big Christmas dinner and invited Vince and his latest lover Steve, who was nineteen and had no conversation but appreciated good food. He must be great in bed, Frances decided. One penalty of having Vince for a friend was putting up with the beautiful but dumb boys he picked up in the bars. Fortunately, they moved in and out of his life fairly fast — sometimes carrying off his loose cash, TV set, and whatever wasn't nailed down.

There really wasn't much need for talk. Erika kept piling turkey, dressing, and gravy on the plates, urging more of everything on Steve, filling the coffee cups. After pie and ice cream they moved into the living room, bundled in sweaters, and watched television. "Eighteen below, wind factor of forty," the announcer said. Frances said dreamily, "I hope he had a good dinner. It seems terrible to have to work on a holiday."

"The weather will turn after New Year's. It always does."

"I hope so. We talked about moving in June, when the lease is up, but it isn't Greg's fault. His roommate has taken me to school every single day — we couldn't move after that. Besides, even the high rises on the Gold Coast have been cold this winter."

"It'll be easier for you when the cast comes off."

"Sure. The doctor thinks I can manage with just a cane. It would help if everything wasn't either slippery or three feet deep in snow."

Steve roused himself to ask, "How do you keep your foot from freezing?"

"Wool sock with a plastic bag over it."

Steve said distantly, "That's why I won't learn to ski. I had a lover once who was nuts about skiing, but after I saw all those people on crutches, I said uh-uh, no broken legs for me."

"How's school, Fran?" A therapist was the last thing in the world Vince would have wanted to be. A ballet dancer, a collector of antiques, the manager of a good gay bar, a circus clown, even — he said plaintively — the owner of a junk shop, which he was. His interests changed from week to week and were seldom, if ever, related to any skills he had. But his affection for Frances was real, and she knew it.

She said firmly, "It's what I want to do."

Because it was. She rode back and forth with her mind on the next day's assignments, studied the night before while Erika graded papers. She hadn't felt like this for thirty years, not since the grade-school days when books had been the most exciting things in the world. She wondered why she had wasted so much time.

She moved her foot on the hassock, wishing she could scratch her ankle. "Hurt?" Vince asked.

"You can't imagine how the damn thing itches. I've scratched it with everything I could get into the cast, and the more I scratch, the more it itches."

"Like poison ivy."

"I'm going to school on borrowed money, with the neighbors hauling me back and forth, I'm twice the age of anyone in the class, but I wouldn't have missed it."

"They get you a job?"

"They try. And once I'm qualified I can work anywhere."

Steve was looking bored. Having eaten, having listened politely to a kind of music that didn't say anything to him, he was ready to leave. Frances hoped he and Vince would go soon. She was tired.

Erika came in with a tray of steaming cups. She had not only made coffee, she had wrapped little foil packages of left-over turkey and dressing and pie for them to take home. It was good to have plenty, to have something to share. Frances felt guilty for hoping she had saved enough turkey for themselves. They parted with thanks and protestations. "We should have helped with the dishes." "No, they'll wait till tomorrow. I have a week off from school." Steve muttered some kind of thanks.

Frances clumped over to the desk where the presents lay in a huddle of tissue paper and ribbons. She had given Erika a pair of nylons, ashamed of the smallness and triteness of the gift but unable to afford more. Erika had given her Chaire Morgan's *The Price of Salt*, in paperback. Vince's contribution, a wreath with Renaissance angels, hung in the window. They hadn't trimmed a tree, having no place to put one, but the wreath gave the tiny living room a nice, holiday air.

Tomorrow was a holiday; classes were shut down until after New Year's. She would just glance into the book and see what happened to Therese, if she got the job, if she went to bed with Richard. She hoped not. Richard was a pleasant guy, but she had already started to identify with Therese.

She was still sitting there, ignoring the cold draft that crept in around the windows, when Erika came in with sandwiches and coffee. Egg salad sandwiches. "I figured you might be tired of turkey. It's almost nine."

It was true. The windows were pitch-black, a few snow-flakes banging against them. "This is a wonderful book. I've just reached the place where she meets Carol. I hope they get together."

"I'm not telling."

"You read it?"

"I always read books before I give them away. How else do I know if they're the right ones?"

Frances scratched the skin above her cast. "This thing is driving me crazy."

"I shouldn't have let you do so much."

"All I did was sitting-down things."

Erika handed her a sandwich and a mug, set the tray on the desk, and balanced herself on the hassock beside Frances' cast. "It's been a nice day, hasn't it? I didn't like the idea of Christmas when I first came to this country. It's supposed to be a Christian holiday. But it's a folk holiday here." She patted the cast. "For families."

"Well, we're a family."

"I'll wear my nylons the first day of school, for good luck."

"When we get rich I'll buy you something terrific." Knowing that Erika didn't care about clothes, never would, what she valued was the love they represented. She wore her skirts and plain blouses like a uniform, and changed into jeans as soon as she got home.

They munched in companionable silence. Finally Frances said, "Do you suppose it will ever get warm?"

"Wait till July. The tar in the sidewalk cracks will melt, and heat will come up in waves, and we'll go to the park to cool off." Erika pulled her sweater up around her neck.

"Adversity does develop new skills. We've learned to make love under three blankets and a couple of coats."

"I prefer the old-fashioned way. I like to see what I'm touching."

"Will you be able to get around when they take the cast off? Sometimes people have trouble balancing."

"I'm not going to let anything stop me."

Erika carried their cups into the kitchen. "How would you feel about going to bed?"

"I could be persuaded."

It was not only the thought of making love that sent her clomping into the bedroom, where Erika was getting out of her slacks and shirt. Making love was wonderful, sometimes it was magical, even when the plaster cast lay there like an intrusive third person. It could be life-giving. But it was only part of their life together. They had cooked a holiday meal and entertained guests — she felt tolerant of Steve now that he was gone — and sent them home with good things to eat. Their bed was a shrine to what they shared, but so were the folding trays from which they ate and the little stove with one burner that didn't work.

She didn't know any words for this recognition. She got into bed and waited for Erika to chain the kitchen door and put out the light. She lay thinking partly about Erika and herself, partly about Therese and Carol.

EIGHT

"We never see each other any more," Frances complained.

Erika looked at her. It was no time to say, "I told you so," or "You set up your own schedule," or, "You knew how it would be when you started this rat race." The words were in her eyes, though — or maybe I'm projecting, Frances thought. She said sullenly, "I don't mind being tired all the time, it's just that we never seem to do anything together."

"You're crying."

"I am not crying. I never cry."

"All right, your eyes are sweating."

"Sometimes I feel like letting the whole goddam thing go down the drain."

Erika said reasonably, "You've been under tremendous pressure the last three years. Now things are letting up a little, the whole weight of it is falling on you at once. You're like the people who hold up under a family crisis and collapse when it's over."

Francis said, "I wish we had more money. I wish we had a bigger apartment."

"That's next on the agenda. Look," Erika said, "you don't have to keep on doing two people's work, going to school and working. You got the first job you applied for. If we had some money we could go somewhere for a month, but we don't. Can't you get more rest at home?"

"I know I'm unreasonable."

"You're human."

Frances said abruptly, "I stopped in to see Helen this morning."

The word *cancer* hung on the air. Erika kept her face impassive. "What did she have to say?"

"Menopause. Good old change of life." Frances smiled, wanly. "I don't know why I feel so surprised. I'm forty-five, median age for it, or something."

Erika's laugh was a little forced. "It's hardly ever fatal. Are you having hot flashes?"

"I'm having something. I start sweating suddenly. But the thing is, I feel so depressed, everything seems so far away and meaningless. Helen says the same as you, it's the release from tension. I had a checkup before I started the job —there's nothing wrong with me."

Erika put sustaining arms around her, but got no response. "Look, you're going to make one hell of a therapist. And we're going to have more money from now on. I don't suppose we'll ever be rich, but we can buy a book once in a while, or go to the theater."

"Or buy a steak."

"What's the matter, don't you like my soup?"

"Your soup is great, but I'd like to go into the A&P just once and not have to think twice before I buy. I'd like to have an éclair or, I don't know, a fudge sundae once in a while."

"You never eat dessert."

"No, but I'd like to be able to."

"Once we're affluent, you'll be homesick for the good old days when we worked our asses off and were always in debt."

She hoped she had diverted Frances' thoughts into a less worrisome channel, but Frances pulled away from her and sat down on the sofa. "Helen says menopause is a normal biological process and women who work outside their homes have fewer symptoms than housewives. It's an occupational disease of housewives, they sit around and drink coffee and talk about their symptoms."

"Did you ask her about taking hormones?"

"Only in extreme cases, she says. Nobody knows what the long-range effects are likely to be."

"It's nice to hear a doctor admit there's something she doesn't know. Most of the male ones think they're God."

Helen Menzies had served in the Korean war, come home and gone to school on the GI Bill, and emerged with a lasting

hatred of war and disease. She had a sharp tongue and a reper-
toire of dirty stories that made her a hit at Sunday-night sup-
pers. Erika was sure she was a lesbian. Frances said, "You think
everybody you like is a lesbian." Now Erika said, "It's a good
thing you're not a psychiatric nurse. You'd have all the symptoms."

"I've been having a few on my own. Night sweats. panics.
I sit up and look at you sleeping and wonder what I'd do if you
left me."

"I have no intention of leaving you."

"You might die."

"Not until I have to," Erika said firmly. "Why don't you
wake me when you start getting those idiotic ideas? Then I'd
feel free to wake you when my turn comes."

There was a small thud outside the door. Frances got up
and brought in the mail. "Two ads and *The Ladder*." She dropped
the brown envelope into Erika's lap. "I wonder how many other
dykes have no other contact with the gay world? People in small
towns, in vulnerable jobs."

"That's us you're talking about."

"Would you join the Daughters of Bilitis if they had a branch
here?"

"The more affluent and respectable we get, the more important it seems to stay under cover. I know half the people at
the hospital are gay. Maybe not half, but a good many, more
than the one in ten they talk about. They just don't admit it."

"We're lucky to have Vince and Philip and Greg. I'm going
to hate to move."

"They know we need a bigger place. There isn't room to
breathe here."

"Oh sure, they know that, but just the same . . ."

"Why is it every time three or four gays get together, they
start talking about coming out? Hardly anybody ever really does
it, they take it out in talk."

"Well, society's still jumpy even about heterosexual relationships. That's why I admire the young kids who simply
live together. They're up against a lot of opposition, a lot of it."

"I keep feeling as if I should be doing something," Francis said, "but I don't know what."

"Let's get out of the house. I think you're having cabin fever. Let's see if the real estate agency has anything lined up for us, and then let's go to the movies and stay downtown for dinner. That's not very exciting, but it would be a change."

"The meatloaf?"

"It'll keep."

"All right, why not?"

One small crisis passed, Erika thought as they changed their clothes and checked their wallets. You solve one, and two more pop up to take its place. That's life.

The real estate man came up with several likely sounding prospects, perhaps because they had been so explicit on their first visit. "We don't mind paying a hundred and forty a month, but we expect something for it. Enough electric outlets, a decent refrigerator, and regular garbage pickup." He was in a competitive business and knew it; if he didn't have what they wanted, they would find it somewhere else. These were professionals, a teacher and a hospital worker; they would be reliable tenants.

"Listen to this. Hundred and fifty, parquet floors, working fireplace, garden apartment—"

"If that means basement, we don't want it."

"No, no, ground floor, I checked this one out myself." They exchanged looks; he was supposed to check them all. "Dining alcove, full kitchen, coin-operated laundry right in the building. One block from a bus line and the Presbyterian Church, three blocks from St. Mary's. Garage space is fifteen a month extra. You pay your own utilities, of course."

"We might look at it," Erika conceded.

"It's still available, but we've had several offers."

"They always say that. If they had a live offer it wouldn't be available."

The place looked all right from the outside: two big trees in the front yard and a waist-high wall around it, a row of floodlights promising nighttime security, a pleasant tapestry brick

facade. "If they don't mind our being women," Frances said
as they looked. "If they only don't think we're lesbians."

"If they're not anti-semitic, while they're at it."

Frances was holding the agency card. "This man's name
is Feldman."

Feldman himself answered the door. "You're lucky. I came
over to see the people upstairs, they're having a little problem
with the shower. I try to keep everything in good condition."

"You're the manager?"

"I'm the owner. I have a good caretaker, divides his time
between this building and one I own on Oak Street, but I try
to handle some things myself." He was about fifty, bald, and
nervous-looking. Frances felt a pang of loneliness for Greg.

They followed him into the building.

"Built-in bookshelves. They would hold thirty books at the
most. Thank goodness we have a bookcase, Frances thought;
it will fit between the front windows. "There's room for a table
in the alcove." A small table, right for two. "People are crazy
about the fireplace. I have the chimney cleaned every summer.
You can store your wood in the utility room." Okay if the other
tenants were honest, fireplace wood being in the same class
as gold or uranium, a luxury for millionaires.

Still, it was the fireplace that decided them. It was brick
in a hundred shades of red and rose and orange, a straight rise
from floor to ceiling, with a stone hearth that extended well
into the room. They could visualize themselves on a fur rug
in front of dancing flames — not that they had a fur rug —
making love or just relaxing after a day's work.

They tore themselves away and inspected the bathroom
(pink fixtures and an etched shower enclosure) and the bedroom (their combined wardrobes would fill one corner of the
walk-in closet) and the utility room, which was right behind
their apartment and could be reached through their kitchen
door. "This is the garbage chute." Galvanized metal, running
the height of the building. "Pickup every day, the upper floors,
it's accessible from the hall." They were to remember that later,
when Saturday night parties upstairs ended in the hilarious

pitching of beer cans one by one, "Each apartment has one day to use the washer and dryer."

"This is my favorite apartment." Likely. "Now I'll need the first month's rent in advance, and of course a month's rent as security deposit. I'll have two copies of the lease for you to sign—I'm a lawyer, you don't have to worry about that." That figured, an apartment building was a good tax shelter. "When would you want to move in?"

"We'll have to talk it over."

They talked it over on the bus, on the way downtown, but they both knew there was no resisting that fireplace.

"We'd have about sixty left in the bank. Could we manage?"

"We'll eat rice."

"What would we do for furniture?"

Erika was calm. "Remember that friend of Phil's who went to Australia? All his stuff is in Greg and Phil's garage. I think we could get it cheap. There's a three-quarter bed and spring and mattress, a couple tables, and a big chair. We wouldn't need much to start."

"You make it sound so easy."

"We're on the way up," Erika pointed out. "I've taught in this system for three years, I have tenure. You'll never have trouble finding work if things don't go well at City. Though why shouldn't they? Just because we've both had a rough time in the past, that doesn't mean it will always be that way."

Frances reached for the bell cord. "All right."

"All right what?"

"Let's skip the movie, catch the next bus back and sign the damned lease. Do you have your checkbook?"

Mr. Feldman was still there. Waiting for them, Erika thought. He had the lease forms ready to fill out and sign. "Security deposit's refundable when you move out, minus any damage you've done to the apartment." Erika had a fleeting mental picture of Frances charging through the living room with a hatchet, chopping window frames and demolishing the fireplace. "What do they mean, damage?"

"Do you really feel like eating out?" she asked when he had left and they stood in front of the fireplace with two sets of keys and a copy of the lease.

"I'd just as soon go home and take a look at that furniture. Do you suppose they'd sell it to us on easy terms? We can't pay for anything now."

"You know Greg. Anyway he knows we're honest—if we weren't, he wouldn't have any trouble finding us. And you have a payday before the end of the month. We can make a down payment."

"Erik, do you ever worry about anything?"

Erika's own opinion was that she had done so much worrying in the first fifteen years of her life, she'd used up her quota. She pushed the thought away. "Sure, I worry about you. A little, old dried-up female with hot flashes."

"I read somewhere that women are sexier after menopause."

"You'll have to prove it to me. Just leave me enough energy to get moved, that's all."

NINE

An elegant facade doesn't necessarily mean opulence within. Still, Frances wished they could afford a professional mover with a big, powerful truck and three or four big, powerful men. What for? Erika wanted to know. To carry in the concert grand?

What they had was a pickup borrowed over Sunday and Vince, looking more pixyish than ever, to help them carry in their boxes and armfuls of clothing. They looked nervously at the windows of the other apartments, but if anyone was watching, no curtain twitched. They arranged their few pieces of furniture, had hamburgers and Coke sitting on the parquet floor in front of the cold fireplace, and took turns scrubbing up in a bathroom considerably more luxurious than any they had ever shared. A real Ollenfield bathroom.

Erika was invited upstairs to have a drink with the three young women who lived overhead while they looked for their screwdriver. She came back to report that they were sitting on plastic egg crates and using an old camp locker for a coffee table. "They don't have any beds, either, just two mattresses on the bedroom floor. Though I must say they have a lot of books."

"Maybe they don't have any money."

"They all work. Sylvia was one of the leaders in the Chicago teachers' strike last year. Now she's blacklisted, so she's a cocktail waitress. I don't know what the others do. They must have some money, they go to the singles bars every Saturday night. They invited us to go along."

"I didn't know Waubonsie had a single's bar."

"The Calico Cat, on Hatfield Road. I suppose they put it outside the city limits to keep the law away."

"Well, you could try it," Frances said. "And pick up a man and bring him back here, or go to his place."

"Would you go to a lesbian bar if there was one?"

"Once, to look it over. Not for cruising, necessarily. We're hopelessly square."

"We're getting old."

Erika frowned. "Middle-aged, maybe. I don't mind that."

"I sort of look forward to being old. A fire on the hearth and a kettle steaming on the stove—and a cat."

"Cats make me sneeze."

"That's right. I forgot. A tank of guppies and snow drifting past the window."

"And bifocals and arthritis," Erika finished. "I'm not in any hurry."

It was a warm evening, but they had built a fire of waste paper and a broken-up crate just for the pleasure of it. A real fire, on their own hearth. The women at the hospital had given Frances a moving-in present, a black iron stand with a poker and hearth brush and a little shovel for the ashes, and Erika had brought home a box of some chemical that turned the flames blue and orange and green. She sprinkled a pinch of it on the fire and stood watching. "Sylvia says they bring home wood from buildings that are being torn down. You have to go after dark, when the work crew isn't there."

"They used to have wooden packing boxes. I had a dressing table made of orange crates when I was in college, with a little curtain around it and a mirror on top."

"Not any more. You can hardly get cardboard cartons now." Erika yawned. "I put ours in the storage room. Someone will need them sooner or later."

They had a sagging rocker, a large club chair from Catholic Salvage, the TV trays from which they had eaten for the last three years, a desk, and a couch with a homemade cover that didn't hide its sags. In the bedroom, a three-quarter bed and a chest of drawers. "We'll buy furniture when we can afford it," Erika said firmly. "When school starts and my checks begin coming in, we can buy a table and some chairs. A nice match set we can paint, maybe."

"We could have bought them on credit if we'd kept those cards." The bank where they cashed their checks had sent both of them little plastic cards to be used like cash—they were promised almost unlimited purchasing power. Erika said, "These things are even worse than charge accounts because you can use them anywhere. People buy stuff they don't need and can't afford because it feels like getting things free. Then they have to pay for everything, with interest." She stopped and considered, "I suppose if you have a car it's handy for buying gas."

"What's the matter, they won't take cash any more?"

"Have you ever counted the cars lined up at filling stations? Or noticed how many people make the news because they've been held up in one?"

Frances said soberly, settling into the rocker, "It's funny. When I married, Bill had charge accounts all over town, and I used them and took it for granted. The first year—but I was so excited about being married, and then I got pregnant almost right away, and after that I was so miserable that owning things didn't seem to matter. Now the idea of going into debt scares me."

"Don't worry, we're not going to be corrupted by wealth or debt, either."

They had returned the cards to the bank with a polite note of refusal.

Erika had found a summer job in one of the better department stores, selling blouses and lingerie three days a week; the Waubonsie schools still paid on a nine-month basis, leaving teachers to live on savings or find supplemental employment from June through August. On her days off she did the housework, which didn't amount to much, and most of the cooking. "I've always wanted a wife," Frances said. "Now I've got one."

"Not for long. Make the most of it."

"Peggy and Dolores said they might drop in. Shall I go out for beer?"

"Let them drink coffee."

"I'm still surprised that they came out to me. Peggy was loaded, she'd been out for a three-martini lunch, or she probably wouldn't have. Not that I didn't know."

Erika said firmly, "It's always a mistake to work in the same place as your lover."

"You don't like Dolores."

"I don't dislike her. The femme-butch thing bothers me, always has. And then she's not overloaded with tact. Does she stomp at work?"

"She's a good nurse. It's pretty hard to stomp in duty shoes, anyhow."

"Oh, hell, a couple of six-packs won't break us. Go on, you can go down to the corner while I find some paper napkins. Isn't it nice to have a real table?"

Frances hovered in the doorway. "She asked about you. Are you a butch? She wants to know."

"How do I know? What would you like me to be?"

Frances scowled. "I was a femme for Bake, I suppose."

"Go. Don't stand there talking about nothing."

Erika made her way into the kitchenette, wondering. What is this femme-butch stuff, really? An imitation of heterosexual marriage in the old days, the days when women were supposed to be subservient and men were supposed to be bossy. But that was European, it was never that way with Americans — not until they got rich enough and citified enough to keep their women as pets. In the early time, women had to be partners to survive. And now gay people have taken it over and they're about fifty years behind the times. What foolishness.

When do we start making a culture of our own?

I suppose I was "butch" for kate, at the beginning anyway. And for Martha? She was more mother and teacher than lover. And for those girls who came home with me one time and gave me some forgetfulness when I needed it? Well, I was small and slender and had fair hair, so the butches were attracted. What does it mean? We are all women.

She was in no frame of mind to welcome Peggy and Dolores when they rang, but there was no one else to do it so she put on a hostess smile. "Come on in. Fran's gone out for beer."

"Hell, she didn't have to do that. We can drink coffee."

"We like something cool too."

"Well, what have you two been up to? Are you getting settled?"

"Talking about furniture mostly. We need everything."

"For chrissake, don't spend a lot on furniture. It's the biggest hassle when you break up, that and who gets custody of the cat."

Peggy winced. "I like your place. That fireplace!"

"We're crazy about it. We had to build a little fire the first night, ninety in the shade, just to see what it would look like."

Dolores was not to be diverted. "I know you don't think you're ever going to split up. You've been together three or four years, haven't you? But you never know. Someone comes along, and boom."

Erika said frostily, "I'll worry about it when it happens."

Frances came in with two six-packs, greeted them quietly, and went to the kitchen for the church key. Erika said, "Excuse me a minute, I'll see if we have anything to eat."

Dolores wandered around the room, looking at the books and records in their improvised cases, taking a good look at the cheap print of Van Gogh's *Sunflowers* that Erika had bought from Vince. "I don't suppose they've got any country and western. God, imagine living with a schoolteacher who listens to Bach."

Peggy said defensively, "I like classical music myself."

Frances came in with beer and glasses, a plate of cheese and crackers, and a jar of peanut butter. Erika said drinking from a can strangled her. She had never learned to drink pop from a bottle. "It isn't very fancy."

Maybe if we're dull enough, Frances thought hopefully, they won't stay long. All right, they're sisters. Colleagues, too. Two reasons for being nice to them. But in a few minutes Dolores will ask why we don't get a color TV, and then she'll say something macho to hurt Peggy's feelings, and I'll see Erika wanting to throttle her.

Don't we have a right to be selective, the same as anybody else? I resented having to entertain the Wives. Why should I put myself out for two dykes I don't much like?

Frances popped her can of beer and settled down on the couch, which, as usual, was cluttered with things waiting to be put away. They couldn't stay forever, and when they were gone, she and Erika would finish their first Sunday in the new place making love. Maybe they would bring a blanket from the bedroom and settle down in front of the fireplace, with a few pieces of paper burning to cast a glow over them. It wasn't firewood, there wasn't any fur rug, but it was worth waiting for.

TEN

By the end of their first year in the garden apartment (no garden), it was hard to remember the sequence of events.

Three Americans landed on the moon and came back to earth, to be greeted with bales of newsprint and tons of ticker-tape confetti. "All those trees," Erika mourned. She had joined the Sierra Club and worried about the environment.

The astronauts seemed, eventually, less important than the Saturday night parties of the women upstairs. They did, as they had bragged to Erika, go to the singles bars, but they didn't stay there. They came back around midnight with an odd collection of young men and women and some not so young. All right, if that was what they wanted. But there followed five hours of light music—she supposed it was music, Erika said sourly —yelling, laughter, furniture being dragged across the floor, and finally, the exodus of the entire party to the hall, to throw the empty beer cans down the garbage chute. After that climax the guests left with loud goodbyes, and Frances and Erika could go to sleep just as the sun began to streak the eastern sky. "A good thing we don't go to church," Frances said, pulling the blankets up around them. "I spoke to Sylvia about it. She just looked at me."

"We could tell the landlord."

"He wouldn't pay any attention as long as they pay their rent."

"We could buy earplugs." But they never did.

Eventually Sylvia was raped by one of the disco habitués and the other two left, unhappy about the publicity; the rapist had called the newspapers to brag. "High, probably," one of the roommates said. There had been a routine call from the police, lights revolving and sirens shrieking. Mr. Feldman had left his law office to counsel silence, but Sylvia had given a full description of her assailant. None of them had ever seen him before and they didn't know his name. Sylvia was the last to leave. She said she couldn't pay the rent all by herself.

The garden apartment was turning out to be less than the home of their dreams. The fireplace did work, and kept them happy and impoverished — a dollar for a bundle of ten little sticks. The regular heating, which was supposed to issue from a grid of metal pipes just under the ceiling, was less reliable. There were storm windows of a sort, but they rattled in the least breeze. The reverberating garbage chute was a nuisance, and, seldom emptied, probably a health hazard. Erika saw a fat rat scuttle across the floor of the laundry. The hose to the washer froze, and Frances had to carry their wash four blocks to a laundromat. As for the garden, nothing grew there except some scraggly grass, although Waubonsie had been built on good, black prairie dirt and there was hardly a house but had shrubs and a vegetable garden.

That was the year they subscribed to the daily paper — there was only one — instead of picking up a copy now and then from a coin-operated box. The Ollenfield name leaped up from the page and hit Frances in the face as she drank her coffee one frosty morning. Mrs. Robert Ollenfield had given a party in honor of her daughter's second birthday, with ten little guests and their mothers in attendance. Frances handed the paper silently to Erika, "Okay, so you're a grandmother. So what?"

"Two years, and I didn't know. It seems so strange."

"Well, neither of us reads the births column."

They were a little shaken, just the same.

In a town of sixty thousand, it seemed strange that they had never seen Bob or Mari — coming out of a store, crossing a downtown street, emerging from a concert at the small local college. Frances no longer looked around apprehensively when she visited the public library. "We move in different circles," she said hopefully.

Erika got a small salary increase, not quite enough to make up for the rising cost of everything. Mr. Feldman announced that there would be no decorating done, as he was losing money on the building. Their apartment didn't need anything done to it, but Erika made a pro forma protest. The lease, drawn up by Mr. Feldman himself, specified that they were entitled to one hundred dollars' worth of renovation a year.

"Like hell he's losing money," Frances said. "If he was, he'd find some way to throw us out. Or burn it down." There had been a spate of apartment house fires and the papers were suggesting, not too delicately, that it might be arson. Burn the building down and collect the insurance.

"Just so he evicts us first."

Their lease was up at the end of June. When school let out, Erika spent most of her mornings—she was selling, afternoons, in a rather elegant candy shop—looking for another apartment. It was discouraging. Waubonsie was a small city of one- and two-family houses; apartments were either tacky, for poor drifters, or impossibly ornate and expensive, for executive types.

"There's something called a condominium. You buy the apartment, but there's a big down payment—thousands of dollars. That lets us out."

"What happens if you want to sell it?"

"Oh, they have all kinds of restrictions. It's worse than renting."

"How can you own an apartment if you don't own the ground it's built on?"

"It's a fraud, to get the big down payment. Gyp deal."

Condominiums were out.

Mr. Feldman had been pushing for a new lease since April. They kept putting him off. Finally Frances located a half-house with a yard and garden. "Sounds nice." Erika approved. They went to look at it.

The half-house had originally been the back part of a whole house, built around the turn of the century for a large family. The owner was a small, bent, sharp-eyed, old lady who probably didn't want to bother with renters but needed the money. Her face lightened when Erika said, "The yard is beautiful. Could we have a garden?"

"You both single ladies?"

Frances said primly, "I'm a widow." Erika looked surprised.

"You see, I'd really rather have a man. Men are so nice about fixing things, and I feel safer with a man in the house." Mrs. Sanders looked embarrassed. "I had two young ladies once. They seemed so nice, but then I found out they were *like that*."

Erika swallowed hard. "Like what?"

"You know, abnormal. Attached to each other. I know there is a lot of it around, but I'd really rather not know about it."

Erika said politely, "Well, thank you anyway." Her cheeks were pink, but she kept her cool until they were out on the street. "The damned old bitch," she said. "Are we abnormal?"

"Some people might think so," Frances considered. "We might as well stay where we are for another year. It's quiet since those types moved out, and nobody bothers us."

Erika said wistfully, "I'd still like a house."

"Who's going to cut the grass? Shovel the walks? Fix the broken pipes?"

"What we need," Erika said, "is a butch. I'd really like to live where there isn't any snow to shovel.

"Florida?"

"Too touristy. Some place hot and dry."

"An oasis in the Sahara."

"Idiot."

They signed a new lease, but with less enthusiasm than they had felt a year earlier. One more compromise in a world full of compromises.

Frances felt better. Helen said she was having an easy time of it; she didn't think so, but at least she had none of the memory lapses and deep depressions she had heard other women describe. Working with other people's physical problems all day, she thought, made her feel well by contrast. Because there were only two hospitals in Waubonsie, City got a sample of everything: postpolio, postsurgical, accidents, multiple sclerosis, drug cases, birth defects. "You name it, we've got it," Dolores said cheerfully. Erika asked, "Doesn't it make you feel depressed?"

"Not when I can do something about it," Dolores assured her.

The weeks slipped past. A little monotonous, perhaps. Erika insisted that she like monotony. "I've had enough excitement for one lifetime. Let's go into the sunset hand in hand."

"Don't count on it. Monotony, I mean. Hand in hand is fine."

"The paper says the French are getting out of Vietnam. Our military advisers are staying. It isn't over yet, what they've been doing there."

"Never mind Vietnam. I don't even know where it is — somewhere in Asia, isn't it? Come to bed."

ELEVEN

"Did you ever hear of a place called Stonewall?"

"A person," Frances corrected. "He was a general in the Civil War, I think."

Erika bent over the pages of the *Advocate*, spread out on the dinette table. "Not this one. This one's a gay bar in New York City — Greenwich Village. The police raided it last night."

"That's nothing new. Even the women's bars — I was in Karla's once." Frances stopped abruptly. That was a night she didn't want to remember. "Mostly it's the men's bars. The plainclothes cop comes in and leaves a joint on the washroom windowsill, and his buddy finds it and books them on narcotics. Or it's soliciting or keeping a disorderly house. The dear, old Chicago *Tribune* used to print lists of names and addresses and places of employment, till somebody took them to court on it."

"Yes, but listen. These guys fought back. The cops dragged some of them out into the street, and they went kicking and biting, and the others came with whatever they could get their hands on, bottles and chairs, and they fought back. They didn't run, or give phony names, or lie. They *fought*." Erika's eyes were shining. "If the Jews had fought like that when the Nazis started in on them, at the very beginning, when they said, 'You can't sit on the park benches' and 'You can't send your children to the public schools' — if they had hit the storm troopers, or shot them — "

"There aren't enough gays."

"There weren't enough Jews either. In Warsaw they fought back. Of course, they got killed anyway, but if they had started sooner, some good gentiles might have helped, maybe." In her excitement, she swept the newsprint sheets to the floor. "Our people are fighting back."

"I thought you were all for nonviolence."

"For nations, yes. Wars are for power and profit. You know why we're in Vietnam — oil and minerals and access to China. It doesn't have anything to do with communism, but if someone comes to the door and tries to kill me, I'll grab the butcher knife and go after them."

I believe she would, Frances thought, amused and impressed. Small, thin Erika with the soft voice and the dreams that still roused her from sleep and left her shaking. Frances shifted to safer ground. "I didn't know you could buy the Advocate in Waubonsie."

"Vince's new boy subscribes."

"That's a switch too. I never knew Vince to have a boy who could read and write."

"A lot of people are getting politicized these days."

"You sound like the lavender women. They won't have anything to do with any men or straight women, or most dykes. They're going to end up with two women sitting in opposite corners muttering to themselves."

"We've only known those two who stayed with Dolores, and they were all talk and no action. They can't be typical. Besides, in any good movement there's always a lunatic fringe — look at all the innocent people they killed in the French Revolution. Or the kulaks in Russia. It takes a while for things to level off." Erika bent to pick up the scattered sheets. "Excuse me while I get down off my soapbox."

"You'll be speaking at rallies if you don't watch out."

"You can pretend you don't know me."

"I'll know you all right."

"Now listen for a minute," Erika said. "Do you want to stay in Waubonsie all your life?"

"Not really. If something better came along I'd take a good look at it. What is this, daydream time?"

"Two years in this apartment. Okay, it's not a bad apartment but it could be better. Also, it's cold here in the winter. Also, we haven't talked about it, but you know, one of these days you'll be walking down the street and you'll bump into one of your ex-relatives. Embarrassment all around. I'm surprised it hasn't already happened." She folded the paper neatly and carried it into the living room. "Don wants this back. Sit down, relax. I've got something to tell you."

Frances took a place beside her on the lumpy davenport. "Never mind being diplomatic. Let's have it."

"How would you feel about moving to Arizona?"

"Why Arizona?"

"Well, it has sunshine and roadrunners and cactuses — "

"Cacti."

"It's warm in winter."

"Granted, but I wouldn't give up a perfectly good job to go there."

"How about trading it for a better one? You know Betty Hummel. She has a cousin or something in Tucson. He says the school system is expanding — they've built new school-houses, they've added teachers because everyone's moving to the Sun Belt. This cousin is an assistant principal. BUT — " Erika took a deep breath, "he's leaving to join VISTA, and Betty thinks I could apply for it. You know I've always wanted to get into administration, that's where the chance to make real changes is, and I've taken all those courses and I did a paper last summer for the NEA convention."

"It was one hell of a paper."

"Thanks. They don't seem to mind putting women in leadership positions, like school boards in the middle west, it's closer to pioneer days, or something. So if you think it's a good idea, I'll put in an application. If they're interested, Betty says they'll fly me out for an interview. Of course they may already have someone lined up."

Frances considered. In the eight years that she and Erika had been living together, she had heard more than she really wanted to know about formal discipline, crowded classrooms, intelligence testing, record-keeping, and intransigent parents. What had first seemed a way to earn a living had become, seen through Erika's eyes, a career in which there was plenty of room for improvement. Erika believed the curriculum fostered medi-ocrity and left out both the above-average and the slow learn-ers. "We're turning out a lot of illiterate TV watchers."

"Being an assistant principal would be a step closer to what you want, I can see that. But what about me? I can't just walk out of a job."

"Tucson's full of old, retired people. It must have hospitals."

Frances looked at her lover, sitting primly, ankles crossed, face serious. Good God, she's over forty and she looks about fifteen. But that wasn't altogether true. If you looked closely, there were little, fine lines on Erika's forehead and fanning out from the corners of her eyes. What made her look young was the fair hair which would fade into gray a little at a time, the candid eyes, the firm lines of her small pointy face. "I love you," Frances said suddenly, and got a small smile. "Never mind that, you have to make up your own mind."

"The idea of uprooting myself sort of scares me. I'm getting old."

"It scares me too. But I'd like a chance to see what I can do — nothing big or world-shaking, just one little system. The Southwest is newer — maybe things wouldn't be so formal, maybe they'd be willing to try new methods."

"When would you want to apply?"

"Day before yesterday."

"Good. Is there somebody you can call? Call tonight. It's two hours — no, three hours, we're on daylight savings — anyhow, it's earlier out there. Call Betty's cousin, or someone."

"It might mean cutting our week at the lake to a weekend. I might have to wait for a return call."

"Can we still afford the lake?"

"We can't afford not to go. We're both tired and ornery."

"How do we get out of our lease? We just signed for another year."

"Sherman Kolb will take care of that. There's sure to be a loophole. Think of it — no more freezing winters, no more icy sidewalks."

Frances looked around the dining alcove, which after six years still held its original secondhand furniture but had acquired venetian blinds, drapes, and the longed-for rug, although this place had no fireplace. The rug was not fur but orlon, originally white, now what Frances called ivory and Erika called tattletale gray. "I've never really liked this place. It's so pretentious and phony."

"The landlord is hard to take. You never know when he's going to drop in with no warning. Now that his spoiled kid lives upstairs—"

"I won't call tonight," Erika said slowly, "but I will call tomorrow and see how things stand. We'd better go to bed. We have to work tomorrow."

"That's a poor reason for going to bed."

"You post-menopausal femmes are so horny."

"You're complaining?"

They left the light on in the dinette, because sooner or later one of them would be hungry. It was amazing, Erika said, how hungry love could make a person. "When I write a book on lesbian love I'm going to include a chapter on midnight snacks. I bet that's why there are so many big, husky dykes. They get up at two in the morning and make toasted cheese sandwiches."

Like the garden apartment, like the tiny flat that had preceded it, this place was furnished skimpily and haphazardly. The dressing table was cluttered with things in no way related to good grooming: a paper clip, an open magazine, a flashlight, a coffee-streaked mug. Erika snapped on the overhead light, and the bed came into full view. "We've had some good times here."

"We'll have good times wherever we are. Besides, we may not be going anywhere. This is just a trial balloon."

"You coin such nice cliches."

They had forgotten about Stonewall. They came into each other's arms with a hunger and a delight sharpened by practice. It was going to be one of the best times, one of the times that lasted and deepened. Well, Frances thought, we can sleep tomorrow. She reached up and turned the ceiling light off. "Look," Erika said, "the moonlight is bright as day."

TWELVE

Lake Geneva was cool, blue, leafy, and radiant with little sunshine-tipped waves. It was also clogged with motorboats and crowded with vacationers. Party-goers went home in convivial groups at three in the morning.

But it was cool.

The old lady two doors down, who acted as a rental agent and collector for the firm that owned the cabins, came to collect and stayed to reminisce. "In my day it was nice and quiet here. Folks came for the entire summer—the men came up on the train for weekends and the women and children stayed here all the time. Then they had the church camps —Methodist, Presbyterian, Lutheran—all the way from Lake Geneva to Williams Bay. And revival meetings. You should have heard the singing on Sunday morning! Now you have to drive clear into town if you want to go to church."

She accepted coffee and cookies, took their check, and left, walking carefully in bunioned sneakers.

They were sweaty and tired; they had come by bus to Williams Bay and walked almost two miles, halfway around the lake, to the campsite. "You don't have a car? My goodness, everybody has cars these days," the old lady exclaimed. "We're thinking of getting one," Frances said gently, "but in the city it's easier to take a bus or a cab." Now she suggested, "We'll need a car if we go to Arizona."

"We're not there yet."

Approached by long distance telephone, the secretary of the Tucson school board had said yes, the position was still vacant. They were considering a couple of people for it, and he would set up an appointment if neither of them worked out. She should hear in a week or so. Frances, "The suspense is killing me. Look, there's a flock of little kids all the same size. Must be a summer camp."

"Let's hope so. The counselors probably tuck them in early."

"Let's walk down to the store and pick up some food. See how many dykes we can spot."

"Idiot, this is Lake Geneva, Wisconsin, not Fire Island."

"Want to bet?"

They showered briefly — both taps ran cold — put on clean shorts and shirts, and walked downhill to the store-postoffice-restaurant. "I'll treat you to whatever they have that's wet and cold," Erika offered.

There was a sailboat far out, like a white-winged water bird. The trees made a soft, murmuring sound. Erika said, "Think what this must have been like in the old days. No power boats, no noisy parties."

"Just bears and hostile Indians."

"I was thinking about 1900. Girls with pompadours and shirtwaists, young men in ice cream pants. Mandolins and uku-leles. I bet a lot of people got engaged here."

"There's a cove marked off for swimming. To keep the boats out, I guess."

Erika said wistfully, "I wish we could stay forever."

"I don't, I'm too excited about Arizona."

"It's hard to think about Vietnam in a place like this." For a boy, surely not over nineteen, in khaki fatigues was walking down the path with a worried-looking parent on each side.

"You can leaflet when we get back. Let's get some cold pop."

Erika thought secretly that she might not survive another week in this state of indecision. In this quiet place the effort she had invested in seeming cool looked like a foolish piece of acting. How could she leave the places and people she knew, make a new life somewhere else among cacti and mountains? She said, "Come on, then. We're here to enjoy ourselves."

A crowd of leggy adolescents pushed for turns at the pop machine. Frances waited in line while Erika went inside for eggs and bacon, milk, ice, bread, a selection of canned vegetables, all priced higher than they would have been at the A&P. "You need charcoal?" the cashier asked.

"No, we're in a cabin with a gas stove."

"Nothing like cooking outdoors."

Frances yelled above the teenagers, "Pepsi or Coke?"

"Grape or strawberry, if they have any."

Brown paper sack at their feet, they sat on a sagging wooden step and drank icy soda. "I may be on vacation," Frances said firmly, "but I'm damned if I'm going to walk around sucking on a pop bottle. Besides, there's a refund on the empties."

A pair of young women paused beside them. The tall one said, "You must be the people in number twelve." "Just for the weekend," Erika said, implying that they wouldn't have much time to fraternize. Still, she liked the looks of these two.

"First time here? Enjoy. I'm Connie. This is Barb."

"I see you're a Cubs fan," Frances said, looking at the pushed-back visor cap. Connie smiled widely. "Crazy, huh? They never win. You from Chicago, too?"

"Waubonsie, wide spot in the road."

"Oh, yeah." Connie looked them over carefully. Were they or weren't they? "You ever get into the city? Like, you know, the bars. The Happitime or Karla's?"

"Karla's, my God, is it still there?"

Now you've done it, Erika's look said.

"Oh, sure, the scene keeps changing." The generation gap was obvious; these women were twenty-five at most. "We don't make the bars often. Barb's a teacher and I do graphic design, freelance."

"What do you teach?"

"PE."

And I bet the girls are crazy about her, Frances thought. Barb was freckled, rangy, and cheerful looking.

Erika and Barb moved closer to each other and began talking about teachers' unions. Frances sat looking over the lake. She asked politely, "Have you been here before?"

"This is our third summer. We bring most of our groceries from home—these places are a swindle. Three dollars for a pound of bacon"

"Yes, but we don't have a car."

What are you? Connie's expression wanted to know. Hippies or something?

They walked to the cabins together, single-file along a path slippery with pine needles, and parted amicably. Connie said, "Come over after supper and have a drink. We're in nine."

"We won't stay long, though. It's been a long day."

"Oh sure, we understand." They had all night for making love, didn't they?

Indoors, Erika dropped the groceries on the table. "Now why couldn't I think of some excuse for not going over there? Not that I disliked them, they seem pleasant and might be good friends if we were staying longer."

"We'll stay half an hour, okay?"

Connie and Barb's cabin was identical to theirs and even more cluttered, wet swim suits draped over chair backs, a guitar, water skis, a couple of books, used glasses. Barb cleared a couple of chairs and produced rather weak martinis. Connie said, "It's none of my business, but do you guys really have to go back so soon? It hardly seems worth the trip."

"I'm flying to Arizona Tuesday, for a job interview."

"Where in Arizona?"

"Tucson."

"We know some people in Tempe. I'll give you their telephone number." There it was, the underground at work.

Erika folded the slip of paper and put it in her pocket. "No more, thanks. I'm a one-drink drinker."

Frances, who always meant to stop with one, accepted a second martini — "Weak, though!" — and a puff on the joint Connie rolled. She felt relaxed, maybe too relaxed. Erika gave her a look that could only be called wifely. "We really ought to be going. It was a long bus trip." Not that long, but she couldn't think of any better excuse. "Thanks for everything. We'll be seeing you."

"Better take our flashlight."

"No need, the moon's up." It was, round and richly golden, shedding a magic light over trees and lake, picking out the paths between cabins.

"Feel free to drop in any time. We're just taking it easy for a couple weeks."

"We're late sleepers when we have a chance."

They picked their way along the path, enjoying the night. Frances said, "They probably think we're too old to have sex."

"They've been together a year and a half. They're monogamous, but they don't believe in monogamy. Connie would probably have a fit if anyone got too interested in Barb. That's what we were talking about in the kitchen. They'd like to have a baby by artificial insemination, if they could find a donor who looks like Connie. Barb would have it. She didn't say who would take care of it while they were at work."

"Shouldn't be too hard, this world is full of freckled redheads. Maybe some nice gay guy would cooperate."

"Would you like to have a baby?"

"I've had one," Frances reminded her. "It's not that simple. It would be a change of life baby all right. And who would the father be?"

"Vince. Always ready to be helpful."

Frances choked on a laugh. "Too much like incest. I'm old-fashioned."

"So was Sappho. So was Susan B. Anthony. Those old girls were pretty smart, they knew what really matters."

Frances held the door open. "My turn to be butch."

"Shall we look up their friends in Tempe, if we go?"

"We're not going yet. I hope we will, because it would be so great for you — a chance to do what you really want to. You've come to a kind of stopping place here, I can see that."

The cabin was flooded with moonlight. They left the bedroom shade partway up, since there was no other dwelling on that side. Erika peeled off her clothes. "I hope there's a laundromat here."

"Sure to be." Frances stretched out on the cool sheet. "Isn't the breeze wonderful? I have a feeling I may never sweat again."

Erika sat down beside her, ran a fingertip across her nose and cheeks. "I have a feeling you may. Want to bet?"

It's strange, Frances thought. It feels so new every time. In the moonlight that lay across the bed she looked at Erika's slight body, postponing the delight of touch as a gourmet might put off tasting a delicious dish. Erika, so slight, so frail-seeming, so passionate when aroused—my little love, my little bird.

She kissed Erika's lips, which always felt a little dry and crinkly. Moved her mouth down, over the thin neck and small, firm breasts. Teased the little pink buttons, until Erika moaned and came in a sudden gush. "Me too, me too. Both of us together."

Frances reversed herself on the bed, reluctant to be apart even for a moment.

Together they feasted, cried out, rode the waves of passion to a crest and over; Erika always the first to lie back sweat-slippery and satiated, ready to start again—Frances, as always, slower in her response. Again, until they were tossed up on the far shore of desire and lay clutching each other, in an unreal world of total fulfillment.

The moon was low on the horizon when they finally fell asleep. The lake made a soft, rhythmic sound, the pre-dawn wind blew cool and fresh at the window. Frances settled into the bed, a hand on her love, and fell asleep. Holiday time: they could sleep as late as they liked, have a leisurely meal, go swimming in the lake, rent a boat, or sit under a tree and joyfully do nothing. She knew they would wake and make love again, more slowly, more delicately, before they decided how to spend the rest of the day.

All these times, she thought as she drifted off to sleep, and never the same, never twice the same. Infinite variety, infinite joy.

THIRTEEN

North central Illinois was gone. Part of Iowa had disappeared. Where the white farmhouses and big red barns had been, the groves where families picnicked, the creeks where children waded and caught minnows, the green pastures where cows grazed, the long tracks where night freight trains wailed: gone, all vanished into the past. Thousand-acre fields stretched away into the horizon. Agribusiness had turned the Midwest into a factory for corn and soybeans.

Fifty miles from Waubonsie the land had been stripped, bulldozed, and artificially fertilized. Frances and Erika had not been fifty miles from Waubonsie in a long time, except to take the train to Chicago through a chain of look-alike suburban towns. Now Erika parked the U-Haul beside the highway and looked around in horrified disbelief. "What happened? Why didn't the people fight it? They must have sold their farms — but how can you sell a farm that belonged to your grandfather? Where are the little cemeteries and the big grain elevators?"

Frances said dryly, "Where are the small towns?" All along the highways, pastel, gimmicky row houses built for a fast money turnover stood tight together. The big, old houses with their cupolas and porches, their tree-shaded lawns, had vanished like the farmhouses. Frances shivered. "I'm glad we're leaving."

"Maybe Arizona will be just as bad. It's full of realty companies."

"You can't destroy the desert. At least, I hope not." Erika started the U-Haul. "It's a good thing I never had enough money to go back to Europe. I wonder what Vienna looks like now."

"Full of tourists with cameras."

"Coca-Cola and missile bases. Remember Jeannete in Spain, a couple years ago? Every little *estanco* had a Coca-Cola sign

on one side of the door and a Pepsi sign on the other. All the
blessings of civilization, in a country that makes wonderful
wine."

"I wonder what Fulton is like? They have machinery now
for mining coal, I saw it in a TV documentary, but I guess they
still need people, too. Who owns these ugly fields?"

"Some guy who has been sold a bill of goods by the bank.
Didn't you ever hear it said, 'A farmer who plows with horses
owns his place — if he rides a tractor, the bank owns the place.'
Somebody has a thousand acres and a million dollars' worth
of high-power machinery, and none of it is paid for, and it won't
ever be. When the bank takes the land, they hire someone to
farm it. They don't even raise chickens or plant gardens any
more. It's crazy."

They had started in high spirits, packing everything they
owned into the fourteen-foot U-Haul, collecting a handbook
on campsites and a jar of change for toll roads and emergency
telephone calls. They were going to take their time and see the
country. In the old days, migrants took their plows and live-
stock and moved westward, always westward.

"There's no more west, just Disneyland and hamburger
stands. Where will people go now?"

"Mars or Jupiter, maybe. We've messed up the earth."

"There used to be plenty here for everybody." Erika's face
was stern. It was a bad turn after such a hopeful start; the rape
of the earth had turned their celebration into mourning.

"Let's not be sentimental about the past. Let's think about
ourselves and the future."

"Also unknown." But Erika managed a smile. "I wish we
were there."

"Relax and enjoy the scenery."

They had a picnic lunch in a spot marked Truck Rest Stop.
They used the restrooms, had a drink from the fountain, and
stretched out on two hard picnic benches to relax their cramped
muscles. Frances struck up a conversation with a pleasant couple headed for West Texas to see a new grandchild. The wife
showed off their camper, with some pride. It was a marvel of
compactness and convenience: room to sleep four if the rather

narrow dinette benches were extended into beds, and hookups for electricity and plumbing. "This is the only way to see the country. You ever been out West? We went to California last year. I tell Joe we'd never have to go home, we could see the whole country and never pay a hotel bill."

Joe looked as though he missed Main Street and the guys at the bowling alley. "No way. I'd just soon go south for the winter, but when it comes April I'm going home and put in a garden." It was obviously an old battle, fought out to a truce. For no reason that she could see, Frances felt cheered by the encounter.

Erika, the transplanted European, was fascinated by American history and read the writings of Lewis and Clark, Jefferson and Henry Adams, and Ruth Suckow with almost equal enthusiasm. Frances suspected that she had been thinking of the U-Haul as a latter-day prairie schooner and the American midland as a vast and trackless prairie. She herself was more concerned with the mundane problems, she was over fifty and therefore might not find it easy to get work, they were without savings since renting the U-Haul and putting a deposit on the house Barb's friend in Tempe had found for them through a Tucson contact. They had less than three hundred dollars to last until Erika's first salary check, and the U-Haul had an insatiable appetite for gas and oil.

She felt, but didn't say, that pioneering was for the young.

She relaxed as they rolled along. The day was warm and bright, early July, and their path was mapped out ahead of time. They would cross Missouri, Kansas, the northern edge of Texas, and New Mexico. Frances had been interested in New Mexico ever since she'd read Mary Austin and Willa Cather. Four days, Erika said, three KOA camps. They wouldn't hurry, they would take their time and see what there was to be seen, take time to talk to the people they met. Maybe they could get a feeling of the places where they stayed, a sense of what the country was really like.

They stopped in Kansas, on a grassy space that was one of a nationwide chain of government-approved campsites. On the rim of a fair-sized city, it had an old-fashioned country

look, with a gravel road along one edge and a thick stand of
oak and cottonwood trees. For five dollars they were assigned
a space under a chokecherry tree, with a picnic table and two
benches and a metal grill between their area and that of the
next campers. A concrete building a few yards away housed
showers and toilets, a coin-operated laundry, and a little grocery store where a stout, cheerful woman presided. "You folks
got a tent?" she wanted to know.

"We're going to sleep in our U-Haul." They had arranged
a spring and mattress in the back of the truck, with a chain
across the opening so they could have air and still be secure
from intrusion.

"You can drown in a tent if it rains. You get some real
good thunderstorms out here. We're from Massachusetts ourselves." She rang up their eggs and bread, and pointed out the
ice and charcoal machines. Don't worry about security. We got
two men patrolling the grounds all night, and we get a nice
class of people here."

A quarter moon was rising in the dark blue sky and crick-
ets and katydids were singing in the long grass as they walked
back to their chokecherry tree. Dewy grass brushed their bare
ankles. They lit a charcoal fire and put eggs and hot dogs on
to cook. Erika said, "Even the politicians can't spoil this. Smell
the air!"

They would remember isolated incidents in connection with
states. Missouri was a night storm, thunder rolling on the horizon and lightning zigzagging over the sky, the sound of rain
on the metal roof of the U-Haul. In the morning a drizzle sent
them on their way without breakfast. They drove up a side road
and found, heralded by new billboards, a little restaurant just
opened by a handsome man of seventy. He explained that he
wasn't really open for business yet, then made hot biscuits and
fried a skillet of ham, produced cream gravy, and sat down to
have coffee with them. "No charge, you're my first customers,
it's for good luck." They thanked him warmly and left with a
feeling that they had met a good human being who deserved
to do well. "I haven't had biscuits and gravy since I was a kid,"

Frances said. "If we don't like Arizona, let's come back to Missouri."

In New Mexico, a scorpion wandered into the shower room where Frances was dressing, and sent her scuttling out with her shoes in her hand. It was funny afterwards. In Texas they ordered hot beef sandwiches in a truckstop restaurant and found the meat so tough they couldn't cut it. "But they raise it here!" "Yes, but you saw the steers." Gaunt, slabsided creatures searching food in barren pastures, they bore no resemblance to the contented cattle of the midwest. Texas seemed bare and inhospitable, mile after mile of highway with no human being in sight, no roadside telephones to call the troopers if one were stranded in deadly heat, no layovers, no picnic tables. Frances asked, "What happens if the car breaks down?"

"They find your bones six months later."

"There must be some nice people in a state this size. They have sense enough to stay indoors," was the best Frances could do.

In the high mesa country, above the glitter that was Albuquerque at night, Frances developed altitude sickness and sat light-headed and shaky-kneed while Erika drove mile after mile. They crossed the state line into Arizona with the approval of a pink-cheeked young trooper who wanted to know if they had any fruit or vegetables or animals, and who warned them against damaging cactus. "They're protected by law. It's a four-hundred-dollar fine if you chop down a saguaro."

They were glad to hear it, although it hadn't occurred to them that they might molest the tall, stark-looking plants. What would they do with one?

They slept in the last KOA and got an early start in the morning, curious and relieved now that they were so close to their destination. Frances looked at Erika's set profile. "We'll be all right."

"Of course we will. Look, there's a palm tree!"

"Sure. We're in the desert."

They stopped at the junction of Interstate Ten and a city street, an overpass shadowing them, and looked at each other. "Sorry we came?"

"No. Let's go."

They kissed briefly, while cars rolled past, and drove on slowly to look for the house Barb's friend had found for them. They had left the generalities of the highway behind and were committed to the specifics of a named street, a numbered house. It was a little frightening.

FOURTEEN

The kid at the gas station was all of seventeen, stripped to the waist above jeans, a mop of fair curls, cowboy boots. He loped across the concrete, watched while Erika filled the tank and Frances rolled down the window. "You from Illinois? How do you like Tucson?"

"Too soon to tell. Look, I can't tell anything from this map. Do you have a city one?"

He leaned in to look. "Interstate Ten, see — this is where you are. Where you want to go?"

"Columbus Boulevard." She pointed out the return address on the real estate agent's envelope.

"Okay, you go from here to here, and turn left onto Columbus from Grant. There's numbers on the street signs."

Her puckered forehead smoothed. "Thanks."

"You're welcome, ma'am."

Erika slid under the wheel. "Ma'am! What are we, a pair of little old senior citizens? He could have been un-nice, like the one in Texas. Look, there's another palm tree!"

"You'll get used to them," Frances said. "They're indigenous, like maples in Vermont. Look, there's a saguaro cactus, like the ones they fine you for chopping down. I wonder how you get one for your yard?"

"Maybe it was there and they built the house around it. What's the one with the fuzz on top?"

"How should I know? Do you realize we're right smack in the middle of the desert?"

Erika wiped her face with a crumpled tissue. "I noticed."

"The biggest and most fertile desert in the world. The Chamber of Commerce says so. I always thought the Sahara was the biggest. I always thought a desert was a lot of sand with an oasis here and there. Here's your stoplight."

They swerved into a side street lined with small adobe and block houses, terra-cotta tile roofs, sandy yards. "Looks like Spain, or the Caribbean. From the travel folders, I mean. Look, there's no sidewalks."

"No street lights, either."

"Look, there's a Mexican."

"Considering we're only seventy miles from the border— besides, there are Mexicans in Waubonsie."

"It's not the same."

"This has to be it." Erika motioned at a small adobe set well back from the street, a red tile roof on its slanted porch-top, a big RFD mailbox at one side.

Erika skidded to a stop. "I feel sort of nervous."

"At least there's a driveway. Maybe everybody drives here. Like in the old days they all rode horseback."

A tall, thin man and a tall, rangy boy emerged from the house and came towards them. Erika said, "They look like cowboys."

"Sometimes I'm sorry you ever learned to read."

"What's that square thing on top of the house, like a cupola?"

"How would I know?"

The tall man said, "I guess you're the ladies that are moving into Les's house? I've got your keys. My kid and I'll give a hand with your furniture."

"That's good of you."

"Not at all. Cooler's turned on, thermostat's working, gas and electricity are on. You'll have to make arrangements for the phone. You got a key for this thing?"

Frances was intent on the amenities. "I'm Frances Kirby and this is Erika Frohmann."

"Glad to meet you. I'm Walt Tollefsen and this is Walt Junior. Now let's get some of this stuff inside. You can keel right over in this here heat. A hundred and eight this morning."

A real feminist would do it herself, Frances thought, handing him her keyring. He took a good look at the back of the truck. "You're set up pretty good for camping, here. If you like to camp out, there's a lot of good places in the mountains. See, we're in the middle of four mountain ranges. That's Kitt Peak up there, where the observatory is. They've got the biggest telescope in the world up there. You'll want to go up and see it some time, when you're settled in." He shouldered the mattress, signalled to his boy to take the bedspring, and headed for the back door. Erika followed with a box of dishes. "What's that square thing on the roof?"

"The swamp cooler? Cheaper than air conditioning. Pulls air in, runs it through water, and cools it off. I turned on your fan." He waved at a small wall switch. "You turn it off and cover it up in the fall, put new filter pads in, in spring. Here's your stove and refrigerator. They're clean, just need to be wiped out when you turn 'em on. Walk-in closet. Bathroom. Let me know if you have any trouble with the toilet. It takes a notion to go on running, sometimes. Living room." There were rust and yellow drapes at the windows.

"Can't have a couple ladies hasslin' with the heavy stuff." He was struggling to set up the bed frame, and missed Erika's scowl.

"Here's your heater, this here little panel on the wall. Now you call me if you have any problems, you hear? That's the most of it, I guess. I kind of like tinkering around in a house — me and Junior have lived with my folks since my wife passed away, and my dad won't let anybody fix anything."

A widower, Erika thought, and hoped that both of them looked too tired and grimy to appeal to him. She caught Frances' look and ironed out her own expression. "This is surely kind of you, Mr. Tollefsen."

"Walt. Mr. Tollefsen's my father." He grinned, shaking hands.

They watched the two Tollefsens get into their pickup truck and drive away. "He's a nice man," Frances said. "Do we have to see much of him?"

"He beats having Mr. Feldman pop in when we're in bed or in the shower. Besides, he's too young for us. I doubt he's a day over forty."

"You know what this town reminds me of, what I've seen of it? A nice overgrown village."

"It's doubled in the last ten years. Says so in that little brochure the Chamber of Commerce sent us. Of course," Erika said, "that said top temperature in July and August was ninety-nine."

Frances was pulling the bedspring onto the bed. She straightened up, breathing hard. "Give me a hand with this."

They fought with the innerspring mattress, got it trued up with the bed frame, and sat back on their heels. "The rest is easy — just takes a little time, and we've got plenty of that right now. Tomorrow we'll find a nice supermarket. And a place for used cars. It's obvious we're going to need a car. I haven't seen one person walking."

"We'll really need two cars," Erika said, sitting down on the bed and pulling off her sneakers. "I can take you to interviews this summer, you'll have something before school starts, and we can look into carpools and bus schedules. A lot of people here seem to drive trucks or vans. But one car — definitely yes."

"Tollefsen seems like a nice fellow. Why am I edgy about him?"

"Sexist. Nice sexist — protect the little woman. The little woman's too frail to shove furniture around. I bet we'll run into a lot of that."

"I take it we're safely closeted."

"Well, advancing age is a help. Nobody's supposed to be interested in sex after menopause."

"Is there any point in taking a shower now? I'd like something to eat before we finish unpacking. In fact, I'm likely to die of malnutrition if I don't have something to eat."

"I noticed a lot of restaurants with Spanish names while we were driving over here. Of course that may be for the tourist trade, but we're still tourists. Tomorrow we'll have to turn in the U-Haul and find a bank and a shopping center and all that, but let's just relax tonight."

Frances stood up to pull off her jeans and tee shirt. "I'm headed for the shower. Add a laundromat to your list."

"How's the bathroom? How's the plumbing?" Erika called after her.

"There's sand in the tub, but that's better than Chicago greasy dirt. The cold comes in warm enough to bathe in. I wonder what we drink?"

"Tap water. They yell about not wasting it, but it's supposed to be safe. We'll buy some refrigerator jars."

"Come on in. Share the shower, share the ecology."

Erika stripped and joined her. "I suppose we have towels some place."

"Dry off on your shirt. Or a sheet. Hang it over a chair — it'll be dry before you know it. Did you notice, what we splashed out on the floor has already dried."

They dressed in the first clothes they found and stepped out into the late afternoon glare. There was no one on the street. "Sunglasses," Erika said. "Everybody's wearing them, did you notice? And a couple of those big hats with curly brims. Ten-gallon hats, I guess."

They plodded through the sandy dust. "People must not go out much nights. There's no lights on the side streets. Look, there's a tree with green bark!"

"The grass is sort of gray, isn't it? Not a real greeny green."

They arrived at a shopping plaza, stores ringed around a huge parking lot. Supermarket, hamburger place, laundromat, drugstore, Ben Franklin. "Something like Woolworth's, I guess. Gosh, I'm thirsty."

"There's a McDonald's."

"Definitely not."

"I can fee the skin crinkling on the backs of my legs."

"That's what you get for wearing shorts. Here's your restaurant, if you think we can afford it. Looks pretty posh."

"We can afford it for one time. The question is, will they let us in?"

The place was dark and cool. A smiling hostess led them to a corner table. They charge for the smile, Frances thought; will they take a check if we don't have enough money? The menu card was long and shiny. Frances asked, "What's a chimichanga?"

"I don't know, but I'm going to find out. It comes with sour cream. Anything with sour cream can't be all bad."

The waitress was decked out for the tourists: full skirt, low-cut, ruffled blouse, and more makeup than they had ever seen except behind footlights. Silver and turquoise jewelry clinked when she walked. Erika said, "I'm going to have a nice, cold glass of beer."

"Mexican or American?"

"Mexican."

"You're living dangerously. I'll have one, too."

The waitress said, "I hope you'll like Tucson."

"I hope so too," Frances said.

Erika said, "I already do."

FIFTEEN

The thermometer outside the kitchen window said 105. Erika stepped outside to sample the weather and came back to report that the people next door had an orange tree in their back yard. "With oranges on it."

Frances, spooning instant coffee into pottery mugs, wasn't impressed. "You know oranges grow on trees."

"I never saw them doing it."

"You want bacon and eggs or eggs and bacon?"

"Some people have no soul."

"Some people have their hands full trying to cook on an electric stove. I do despise them. An electric stove has only two settings, cold and burn."

"When we buy a house, we'll have a gas range." It was one of those impossible dreams, like buying a diamond bracelet or having your own swimming pool.

They returned the U-Haul, which had made the trip from Waubonsie without a dent, and applied the refund and their small savings to a little blue Datsun. "Previously owned," the dealer said, making out the papers. Nothing was secondhand any more. Ignoring all the useful things they might have been doing, like washing the woodwork or hanging up their clothes, they drove miles over winding, sandy roads to the Desert Museum and found a microcosm of the great sprawling Sonora. Frances loaded the car with maps and pamphlets. Erika sat in a natural aviary and listened to the songs of unfamiliar birds. "What's the one that goes oo-oo, oo-oo?" "That's a mourning dove," a passing docent told her. "Not where I come from." Frances pulled at her sleeve. "Come and look a the lizards. They're prehistoric, like little dinosaurs."

They walked back to the car on aching and swollen feet. "It's beautiful, but I'm walking on my ankles. We'll have to buy sandals — everybody wears sandals, did you notice? They keep your feet cool."

"Now if I can remember which is a javelina and which is a jojoba I'll be all right. I wonder if there's a Berlitz school here. We're going to have to learn Spanish."

"I have a feeling we'll take it in through the pores."

On the steep downward trip they saw a roadrunner, complete with half-moon crest and the stiff-legged gait they had laughed at in animated cartoons. It stalked ahead of them on the single-track road, in no hurry. Frances said as the car idled, "I have more respect for Walt Disney than I ever did before."

They steered the Datsun into a layover and sat looking across the mountains, blue-purple and mist-circled. "Beautiful," Erika said softly. "Look at the saguaros, hundreds and hundreds of them. They grow, I forget how slow — a tiny bit a year. Maybe some of these were already here when Columbus landed. Do you think that's possible?"

"Sure, but not probable. They get old and die. You can see the skeletons."

"It makes me think about old times when only the Indians were here."

"I didn't expect this when I married a schoolteacher," Frances told her. "Do you know which mountain is which?"

"I know their names. Catalina, Tucson, Santa Rita — what's the other one? Rincon. But I don't know which is which."

"I always thought Maxfield Parrish invented those colors."

"Who is Maxfield Parrish?"

"Romantic painter. My high school teacher thought he was wonderful. There was generally a sexless girl in Greek robes, sitting on a tree branch or perched on a mountain peak or something, and a sort of haze over everything."

"Sounds pretty bland."

"I suppose they were. Cultured people had them in the living room. Magazine covers, back in the twenties and thirties."

The roadrunner had left them. Frances tried not to feel nervous as Erika maneuvered the little car down the mountainside, around sudden curves, alongside sheer drops to the valley below. "The car's a native," she suggested. "An eastern one would never make it."

There were two pieces of mail in the RFD box, an ad addressed to Boxholder and a political circular addressed to Occupant. Still, mail is mail; someone knew they were there. The house, still cluttered, was beginning to look like home. The cooler hummed gently, the refrigerator went on as Frances opened the door. She poured cool water from a grapefruit juice bottle, and they settled down at the owner's dinette table.

"It feels like a new start," Erika said dreamily. "As new as the Honeymoon Hotel, only things look better now. We have made some headway, haven't we?"

"We still don't have any money. I'm going out Monday to look for work."

"I feel too relaxed to care. This is a very relaxed climate, isn't it? There's a whole column of psychologists and counselors in the phone book — how can anyone be nervous out here?"

"Some people would be nervous anywhere."

It was Frances, the next day, who came in from a long walk to say that she had seen an Indian. That he was wearing cowboy boots and blue jeans didn't diminish her excitement. "I know there are Indians in Illinois, but they look like everyone else. This man looked like Sitting Bull. He spoke to me."

Erika, putting books on the shelves, raised an inquiring eyebrow.

"He said, 'Sister, if you're going to walk around in this sun, you better get you a hat and some sunglasses.' "

She also reported that downtown didn't look like much. "Some of the buildings are empty. There's a kind of skid row, cheap hotels and pawnshops and stuff. The businesses must have gone out to the shopping malls. But right behind the old stores there's a lot of little adobe houses that look like they've been there forever, and Mexican people living in them." She stopped to consider. "The downtown stores have the rate of exchange posted, dollars and pesos. The salespeople are all bilingual. If I'm going to work in any kind of a health facility, I'll have to learn Spanish."

She had found the downtown postoffice hiding in an artsy-craftsy labyrinth of gift shops and expensive little restaurants, "I was afraid to explore it—I figured I'd never find my way out. Nothing here has numbers on it."

"I saw the mailman," Erika told her. "He drives a little, sawed-off truck with right-hand drive, I don't know why. Do you suppose they send them to England to be trained? He called me ma'am. So why do we need a postoffice?"

"For buying stamps."

That was the day they got a postcard from Vince, who said that he missed them and it was hot in Waubonsie. "That's what he thinks," Frances said.

They drove out to San Xavier Mission and were delighted with the cathedral, a mix of Spanish, Indian, and Moorish, faded by time and weather. Worshippers lit their candles and said their prayers in complete disregard of the tourists. The souvenir shop offered little bottles of holy water alongside candy made from guavas and cactus fruit. Frances bought a bottle of holy water with a cross engraved on it, admitting that she had no use for it. "It just seems to go with the place."

The mission, located at the edge of the Papago reservation, looked after the well-being of its neighbors as far as possible —operated a school for the younger children and tried to keep the language and culture alive. Erika was horrified to learn that many of the older children were sent out of state to boarding schools where they were de-Indianized; lacking bus fare to bring them home for the summer vacation, families kept them at home rather than face an eight-year separation. "They're the poorest kind of people," the young priest told them. "High infant mortality, twice what it is for Anglos—lots of unemployment, they've lost their holy places and a lot of their land. You think the Chicanos have a hard time? Take a look at the reservation people."

"Harriet Beecher Frohmann visits the southwest," Frances suggested when they were on their way home.

"She was right, wasn't she?"

"It's a good thing you're not a writer."

"It will be interesting to see what the public schools are like. They've been building new ones, but the population is growing so fast they can't keep up. The teaching is bilingual, at least in the lower grades. The man who interviewed me says my kids will be mostly Spanish and black. It's against the law to keep records of race and religion, but of course you can pretty much tell."

"I'm going out tomorrow and start looking for work."

"What's the hurry? I want to drive down to Sonora and see what it's like. It's so exciting, having a foreign country only seventy miles away."

"I don't know why. It doesn't make any sense, but I'd like to have a job before my birthday. Fifty-two—God, I'm getting old."

"I like you old." Erika turned to look at her. There were lines between Frances' eyes, behind the glasses; careful touching-up kept the few white hairs from showing.

"You look pretty good to me."

"It's not how I look, it's how I feel."

SIXTEEN

"How do you like Tucson?"

Frances looked up from her file cards. "Fine. Only that's usually the second question."

"What do you mean?"

" 'Where you from?' Then, 'How do you like it here?' The third one is, 'Hot enough for you?' "

Carol giggled. "Yeah, I guess it's not very original. A lot of people here do come from somewhere else, though. I was born right here, in St. Mary's Hospital." She perched on the corner of Frances' desk, dislodging the unfiled cards. Frances said, "I guess everyone's a native of somewhere."

She gave up trying to work. "It's fine so far. I'm not as spaced out on the desert as Erika is. She says she feels as if she's come home. Or did you mean the job? It's what I was doing before, except with palms instead of maples on the grounds. I've always liked being a therapist — started late, after I knew what I really wanted."

"That's your roommate's name, Erika? I never knew an Erika before."

"She was born in Austria."

"Are you monogamous?"

Careful, Frances cautioned herself. All you need in a job like this is to get chummy with Miss Blabbermouth here. "How do you mean?"

"Oh, come off it. I saw you together in the supermarket Saturday. I can always tell." She giggled. "Takes one to know one."

"There's something sexy about buying potatoes?" Her voice was as cool as she could make it, considering that she was shaking inside. The kid couldn't be more than nineteen. From her

uniform, she was an aide, and they started at sixteen, but even
a sixteen-year-old ought to have some sense.

"I suppose it's the generation gap. You old dykes are still
in the closet. One of these days somebody's going to break your
door down."

"You don't have to do it."

"How old are you, anyhow?"

None of your business, Frances thought. "Fifty-two."

Carol's eyes widened. "Then I suppose you still believe
in monogamy."

"It has its good points. Saves a lot of fights and breakups."

"I think you're attractive, for an older woman."

"Thanks a lot. Would you mind lowering your voice? Or
better yet, go and do whatever it is you're supposed to be doing, and let me get on with my work."

"I suppose that upsets you. I think monogamy's morally
wrong. It's almost as bad as being married. How can you go
through life just loving one person?"

"Practice helps. I suppose you love different people in different ways. There's lovers, and there's friends. When you find
someone who's both, you stay together. If you're lucky."

"I'd like to go to bed with you myself."

Frances looked at her.

"I suppose you wouldn't leave those damned cards for some
other time and come out with me for coffee?"

Uh-huh, she is underage, generally they start by offering
to buy you a drink. "Not if you're going to discuss my personal
life so everyone in the coffee shop can hear."

"You're supposed to be through at four, aren't you? They
don't appreciate it if you work overtime. You'd still be home
in time to have supper with the little woman."

"You sound as if we were still back in the old femme-
butch days. It's so old-fashioned of you."

Carol looked hurt. Frances said, "Well, okay, one cup—I
don't have time for more." So the kid doesn't have any manners, is that a reason for me to hurt her feelings?

She looked Carol over as she dropped her cards into a drawer
and locked the desk. Solid-looking, no makeup, a cap of short,

dark curls. There was something familiar about her, but of course it was a small hospital, they must have passed each other in the halls many times. She said, to change the subject, "You're right about the overtime, but I'm not apple-polishing, I'm still getting into the routine."

They walked out of the hospital, a cheerful-looking sprawled-out building on one level, the outside walls painted in brown and tan and terra cotta. Frances said absently. "Wright said a building ought to look like part of the landscape." Carol looked puzzled. "Wright who?"

"I do hate elevators," Frances said, avoiding talk about Wright.

"I don't mind elevators as long as I don't get stuck alone in them."

"That's what Bake used to say."

"Who's Bake?"

"A woman I used to know. My first lover." She would have bitten her tongue, but it was too late, the words were out. Was she trying to impress this fresh kid? See, Erika isn't my first lover, I've been around. Carol was making her feel elderly and stuffy. And why Bake, rising up like a ghost out of the past?

But of course it was Bake that Carol reminded her of. Same build, same coloring, same low-pitched voice. So what? It's a common type. The human mind is certainly a tricky thing, Frances thought; it will screw you up every time.

"What's so funny?"

"Nothing really."

"We don't have to drive. It's only a couple blocks to the coffee shop."

"Then I'll have to walk back and get the car."

Carol looked critically at the little Datsun. "Is it yours?"

"Mine and Erika's. If we ever get it paid for. She's car-pooling."

"Who gets it of you split up?"

"I'll worry about that if it happens."

"Doesn't it get boring always making out with the same person?"

"Not yet."

"How long have you been together?"

"About nine years. Since 1960."

"Jesus, is she monogamous too?"

Frances turned the ignition key. "The way you keep harping on monogamy, you must feel guilty about not being."

"Turn left here. I keep telling you, I'd like to go to bed with you. Maybe it shocks you to have me come right out with it like this. You'd rather have wine and candles and a fire in the fireplace and all that shit."

"I think you have a case of presbyphilia—liking older women. Maybe you're really looking for a grandmother."

"The hell with that, I like women all ages. You can park here—we're lucky there's room, this is a busy place."

But the room they entered was more than spacious enough for the dozen or so women who sat around, relaxing after their day's work. There was a long no-nonsense bar down the middle and several small tables set around the walls, some good photographs of cacti on the walls; in one corner a checkerboard was set out with a half-finished game but no visible players. Bar? Club? Restaurant? Frances accepted a cup of cappucino and said tentatively, inquiringly, "It's an interesting room."

"They serve dinner from six on. I don't come here very often, can't afford to. It's just I like to go places run by the sisters. We have to support each other."

She looked slantwise at Frances. "You don't have to worry. Nobody will cruise you as long as you're not alone."

"I wouldn't have expected you to mind that."

"Look, I'm not sneaky. I come right out and say what I think."

And how much better it would be if you didn't, Frances thought. She said dryly, "You sure do."

Carol looked embarrassed. "All that old glamor stuff is out of date, I believe in being honest. "

Frances considered. There was surely something to be said for forthrightness. She remembered Bake's old crowd, all that shuttling around from one partner to another, always with the hope of making a lasting relationship this time. The secret meetings, the lies, the accusations, the discoveries, the quarrels, the tearful or angry separations, the arguments over who got the cat and the record collection! Bake had lived with at least three of her barhopping friends. Maybe the kids had found something better. At the very least, they expected less and so were less likely to be disappointed. She asked, "If you were living with someone, would you tell her when you made love with somebody else? Names and places and all?"

"It wouldn't be any of her business. I live with five other dykes on women's land, it's a commune, and right now I'm in relationships with two of them. Nobody cares. It's wrong to be possessive."

"It's also human."

"Because we're conditioned to it. See, it comes from the olden days when women were the property of men. Men didn't have to be monogamous, we didn't own them. We've internalized male values."

Frances sipped her cappucino in silence. She didn't really like it much, she preferred ordinary coffee; it was the phony glamor, she supposed. "I can see your point," she admitted when the silence began to seem oppressive, "but don't you think we should have some options? Women have a right to be gay or straight, even celibate if they feel like it. You can't lay down rules for everybody."

Carol shook her head. "Celibacy is a form of mental illness. Would you go without eating?"

"I might fast for a while, especially if I'd been eating too much and felt stuffed. If you want to think about sex in terms of food, different people thrive on different diets, don't they?"

"Don't you like me?"

One of the impossible questions. If she said yes, of course I like you, the way was open for further exploration of a relationship she really didn't want. If she said no, I don't like you, she was not only being rude but untruthful. She had no reason to dislike Carol—she was beginning to feel interested in the girl as an example of an emerging new generation, She said carefully, "If you're so long on honesty, the answer is that I don't really know you."

"That's what I keep telling you. I want to know you better. So why do you keep dodging?"

Decidedly, she looked like a younger and even bolder Bake. Frances felt unreasonably pleased with herself for having seen it. "What's so funny?" Carol demanded. Frances shook her head. "Nothing. I just thought of something funny."

"I'd like you to see where I live. Why don't you come home with me for supper and meet some of my friends? That's if you don't mind vegetarian food — we have fish sometimes, but not red meat."

"Why not? I could call Erika. I have to be home early, though — tomorrow is a work day."

"Pay phone in the corner. Do you have to account for where you go?"

"It's only courteous to call if you're going to miss a meal," Frances said patiently. "That's ordinary good manners. I'm sure your mother told you that."

Erika, answering on the second ring, sounded a little surprised. "Sure, go ahead. If you're still hungry when you get home you can make a hamburger." From which Frances deduced that she had some experience of collective vegetarian meals.

They went back to the hospital parking lot. Carol had a battered pickup truck; she led the way out of town, Frances following in the Datsun. The truck held a ladder, a length of hose, and some enormous boxes. "We're building on. We've built the whole house ourselves. When we can afford it we'll get some plumbing."

They could have used a level and a yardstick, Frances thought when they pulled up in front of the oddly shaped adobe building surrounded by saguaros. Wright would have found it interesting, Frances thought. It was approached by a narrow dirt path, the only sign that the place was separated from the surrounding desert. "Adobe's cool in summer and warm in winter," Carol explained. "It's cheaper than lumber and we all helped make the blocks." To Frances, brought up in the log-cabin tradition, that sounded sturdy and independent.

The building had started as a square, more or less. Rooms had been added at various angles, each with a small deep-silled window, and the whole thing had been roofed with sheets of tin — not as attractive as tile, but surely practical. At one side was a small weedy garden: Frances identified beet tops and some wilted cabbages. Carol led the way to the door. "We can't afford to irrigate — we have to carry our water about three miles, from a friend who lives on a farm. But we raise good onions and it's good for the spirit to work in the soil."

Frances wished she could give them a few bushels of good Illinois black dirt. They went into a large room with a bottled-gas range at one end and a fireplace on the other, a round table and some odd chairs, and three young women who managed somehow to look alike even though they were different shapes and sizes. All wore patched jeans and rather grubby tee shirts with various legends printed on them. Two were barefoot, one wore boots; all had long hair. Carol said, "Peg, Jodeen, Mountaintop, this is Frances. She works with me. Come in my room, Fran. I want to get out of this damned uniform."

Her room was one of the lopsided additions. The window looked out on sand and saguaro. There was a mattress in one corner and a tangle of clothes on the floor. Carol pulled off her striped pinafore and white blouse and hung them on a hanger, placed it on a nail driven into the wall, and stood naked except for a pair of bikini underpants. Her body was solid and slender, the breasts erect. Frances felt a stir of desire as the girl bent over and picked up a pair of slacks from the tumble on the floor.

Carol moved quickly, threw her arms around Frances and held her close. "We're exactly the same height," she said, pleased. "Kiss me. No, open your mouth and really kiss me." Her lips were insistent. Frances looked towards the open door.

"They don't care, we believe in sharing. We have group sex sometimes." Carol's hands were inside her blouse now. It felt good. Frances stood unresisting for a moment. Then she moved back a step. "Look, this isn't the time or place. And I don't have sex with people I've just met! You can blame that on old age if you want to."

"Some other time, some other place?"

"Maybe. I'm not making any promises."

"Why do you make such a big thing out of it? That's so middle-class."

To Frances Kirby, coal miners daughter, middle-class would have been a step up. To Mrs. William Ollenfield it was a step down. To Frances, Erika's lover—she wasn't sure whether to be offended or amused. It was meant to be a put-down. At least she's not a party member, Frances thought; she could have said bourgeois. "Let's just say I'm not in the mood."

Carol belted her slacks snugly, leaving her torso bare. "You have nice tits, why do you wear a bra? Oh, come on, supper's probably ready."

Mountaintop said, smiling. "I hope you like brown rice. We have it every night."

Frances helped spoon it onto the plates—no pampering the guest. There was broccoli, not raw but not quite cooked either, and a mix of red and green peppers and pinto beans in oil. I'll need that hamburger, she thought. She and Carol and Mountaintop sat on the three chairs. The others—two more women had come in, wearing ordinary slacks and shirts, probably from jobs—sat on the floor with their plates on their laps. There was little talk; apparently eating here was not a social function but a biological one. When they were finished, one of the women washed the plates, dipping them casually into a pan of cold water and stacking them in a plastic drying rack.

They're pioneers, she thought. That's great. They put their money together and everybody shares. I wouldn't be surprised if they all dance naked in the moonlight. Very romantic. But I bet those dishes are greasy.

It was still half-light when she left. With a big yellow moon coming up over the mountain, reminding her for some reason of sheet music seen in childhood. Carol and Mountaintop walked her to the car, "Be careful going home," Mountaintop said maternally. "It gets real dark out here, but I guess you're a good driver."

"I'll be careful." There was something about the accent. "Where you from?"

"Ohio. I'll never go back east—they can keep their snow and ice."

It did get dark quite suddenly, the last light leaving the sky, the bright glow of the moon throwing shapes into dark relief, making a black cutout of the mountains. Cooler, too. She had forgotten to fill her thermos—but then she hadn't planned to drive outside the city limits. Suppose the car stalled? she thought in sudden panic. Oh hell, why should it? Anyway, people will be going to work along this road in the morning.

The desert was vast and aloof, neither cherishing nor harassing the living creatures that made their homes in its long, rocky stretches. You learned the conditions of life that the desert imposed and provided for them as best you could. The desert had seen races of human beings come and go, and it didn't care.

The summer before, a dozen illegal migrants had been abandoned by the "coyote" who guided them across the border, robbed them of their last pesos and left them to die of heat and thirst two miles from a state highway. Nine did die; three were given first aid in a local hospital and sent back to Mexico; the coyote too was found dead of heat exhaustion, a grim justice. No wonder the desert patrol was a major item in Arizona's budget, Frances thought as she parked on a turnoff to watch the moonrise.

The city was spread out below her, a long band of glitter with the sheltering mountains all around. A cool breeze blew in at the half-open window. It was going to be a good night for sleeping.

I am not going to get involved with Carol.

Maybe it was gross and materialistic of her and Erika to have a swamp cooler (rented) and a small heater (also rented and as yet untried) and a small car (partly paid for). But she wasn't about to change her lifestyle, no matter how contemptuous these young things were. She was willing to admit their courage, their determination to be honest, but their truth wasn't hers. Maybe, she thought, there is no absolute truth, but only a multiplicity of half-truths. and this is what makes so much conflict among people who sincerely believe, all of them, that they have the word.

She began thinking of what she would tell Erika about this evening, editing out the brief abortive scene in the bedroom. In their nine years together both of them had had plenty of chances to try other women: Erika had been drawn to a sad-eyed Vietnamese girl in the Waubonsie library.

She felt a stir of lust at the memory of Carol's hard, young breasts pushing against her. Erika would get the benefits of this evening's experience, in a bed with clean sheets, behind the safety of locked doors.

Okay, I'm middle-class. Is anything wrong with that?

She decided that it was just as silly to insist that everyone must bathe as to think that nobody should (but a good deal more pleasant for other people) and on this reasonable, if not very original idea, she reached the city's first stoplight and plunged into its evening traffic.

SEVENTEEN

She did tell Erika, while she munched her hamburger and drank coffee; tried to make a joke of it. She was taken aback by getting, not the amused smile she expected but a long, thoughtful look. "Did you want to make love with her?"

"Heavens, no. Not any more than I want to go to bed with Katharine Hepburn when I see her on the screen. A kind of automatic reflex, that's all."

"Because you're a free person. Nobody has a right to say what you can or can't do. The choice is yours."

"That's all right in theory, but you'd be upset."

"I probably would. The kids talk a lot about how bad it is to be possessive, but it seems to be built into us — or learned very early, maybe. No real way to tell what's instinctual and what's socially acquired. I certainly wouldn't stop loving you if you were temporarily interested in someone else."

"Have you been with anyone else since we began living together?"

Erika shook her head. "Before, sure. You know about Judy, and Martha, and Kate, and there were others that didn't really matter, in the bad time after Kate died. They're not important now. You'd never had anyone but Bake, and if you don't mind my saying so, that wasn't the world's greatest coming-out."

Frances said with a smile, "Loving you seems to be a fairly diverse experience. That's a compliment, in case you don't recognize it. There's so much more to a woman than a cunt and a pair of tits, there's a whole human being. And you're a pretty complicated one."

"But that's what being a lesbian is about. Not just what we do in bed, but everything we share, even cooking dinner or going to the laundromat. It's mental and emotional and social, I guess. The really promiscuous ones, the girls who pick people up in bars — they always seem to be imitating men."

"Carol and her friends wouldn't agree."

"That's their right. Besides, they might tell you they're a sisterhood, they share everything, including sex. You notice she didn't push herself at you until she'd introduced you to her home and sisters."

"You know, she does look like Bake. Was I looking for a way to go back when I went home with her?"

"People do keep looking for their mother or father or first husband, or some movie star they loved when they were twelve," Erika considered. "Judy looked a bit like Katja, who was my first love, in the camp. It never seems to work very well."

Frances put down her empty cup. "Let's go to bed."

So it was solved.

But it wasn't. Carol stayed away, didn't come to sit on the desk in the therapy office or seek Frances out in the cafeteria, and Frances found herself looking for the girl as she went about her work. A whisk of striped skirt down the corridor or the sound of a voice with a midwestern accent quickened her. Of course, she told herself, it's natural to be curious about someone who's interested in you. Be thankful she's not hassling you.

It was a little deflating to realize that Carol had given up her pursuit so easily.

It was about two weeks before the issue was reopened. She was having a light lunch, in the interest of weight loss, when Carol arrived at her table with a loaded tray and an uncertain smile, like that of a punished child who wants to know if his mother still loves him. "Do you mind if I sit here?"

"Not at all. Sit down."

Carol arranged her plate, silverware, and iced tea carefully, not looking at Frances. "The food in this place stinks. The salads aren't bad, though. Generally, I bring something or go out to the health food store. All this starch."

"Institutional food." She saw with amusement that Carol had a heaping plate of spaghetti with a reddish sauce. "I thought you didn't eat meat."

"Half an ounce of hamburger. It's mostly cereal anyway."
Carol poked at the mess with her fork. "You mad at me?"

"No, why should I be?"

"I thought maybe you thought I came on too strong."

"Nothing wrong with that. You might as well say what you thInk — avoid misunderstanding."

Carol said gloomily, "You're so damn reasonable. I hate people who never lose their cool."

"I lose mine, all right. Not often, but then I do I make up for lost time. So why should I act upset when I'm not?"

"You don't like me, do you?"

"Sure I like you. Why wouldn't I?"

"Well, for one thing I've never been involved with an older woman before." She sounded about twelve, and Frances found It hard to keep a straight face. "I don't know how your mind works."

Frances devoted herself to her salad, picking out bits of parsley and laying them along the edge of her plate. Carol said, "You should eat the parsley. It keeps your blood pressure down."

"That's what Erika says. I just don't like the stuff." She added with a smile, "Do I have to conform to someone else's idea of what I should eat?"

"I guess not."

They ate in silence. Frances finished and pushed back her chair in a little clatter of silver and talk from the next table. Carol said in a rush, "Look, I still want to make love with you. What harm would it do?"

"Not any, I suppose." She felt suddenly tired of all this. "All right, you win. But I won't do it with half a dozen other people around."

"Okay. You want me to come to your place?"

"We could go to a motel, but I don't have any money."

"You're kidding. Two women?"

"What do they care as long as you pay?"

"Mountaintop went to one with her friend from Phoenix. It's better if you have cash, though — not credit cards."

Frances thought about it all afternoon. A stupid thing to do; if she had a grain of sense she wouldn't even consider it.

The two of them would be in uniform, easy to identify if anyone felt a malicious curiosity. And over and above that, there
was her own relationship with Erika, which was — she had
no doubt at all — the most important thing in her life. It's crazy,
she told herself.

But five o'clock found her in a small tacky-looking motel,
a row of semi-attached cabins she had seen in movies but never
experienced. Nobody was around. Carol found the manager,
who was taking a late-afternoon nap (probably getting ready
for the all-night hot sheets trade, Frances thought) and paid
him from Frances' billfold. Frances watched while the younger
girl turned on the cooler and turned down the sleazy spread.
The sheets were wrinkled; had they been used before or were
they only badly washed? She said, choking down her nervous
tension, "No candles, no wine, no fireplace," and Carol laughed.
"Who needs it?"

All right, Frances thought in sudden anger, it'll be plain
unadorned sex. She asked for it and that's what she is getting.
As a girl, as a frustrated young wife, she had dealt with half-
knowledge, thirsted for sex and feared it at the same time. It
got girls in trouble. At best it pitched them headfirst into dull
marriages with young men who were and remained strangers.
Yet there was always this fascination, this inner pull to something that attracted while it repelled.

Bake had taught her to love her own body and its responses.
Married to Bill Ollenfield, she had thought, "Is this all there
is — and why all the fuss?" Bake had taught her to like sex, to
be proud of her own growing skill as a lover. Erika — but she
was not going to think about Erika in this place. Erika was home-
baked bread, every day's food, as necessary as air or water. What
she expected from this encounter was the flavor of cake or candy.

What she felt as she pulled off her uniform was self-
consciousness about her body. Not a bad body, not as slender
as she might have liked but not bad for a woman of her age.
There was the trouble — she was no longer young, oh God, she
was middle-aged and she knew it. A sag here and there, a crinkly texture in places that used to be as smooth a satin, Erika
didn't mind, any more than she minded the hairline crack in

her favorite coffee cup. Carol was eighteen and took youth for granted.

But Carol apparently didn't mind either as they fell naked into bed. Well, Peg was homely and Mountaintop was pudgy. Maybe looks didn't matter in this brave new liberated world.

She put self-consciousness from her as they began the slow exciting routine of learning each other's bodies.

She half-expected some new and exotic kind of lovemaking, garnered from the Kama Sutra or passed on secretly from commune to commune by the international youth culture. Would she be able to respond adequately? But after an interval of nipple-nibbling and fingertip exploration, Carol settled down with energy and enthusiasm to much the same techniques Frances had experienced with the other women in her life—the same love she had enjoyed several times a week with Erika, except that it wasn't Erika's dear fragile-feeling body she was holding but that of a total stranger. Never mind age and generational differences, the game seemed to be played by the same rules everywhere. It was fun, it was exciting, her body responded by itself, with the ease of practice; her body took over, and as she reached the peak of sensation she forgot where she was and who was making this miracle of feeling. It was more or less what she had learned to feel with Erika.

Except that this was not Erika. As the excitement receded, as she lay washed up on the shore and the waves receded, she began to feel embarrassed. She wanted to put on her clothes and get out of there.

She held Carol politely for a while and then got up and dressed and drove her back to the hospital parking lot. They parted with a kiss that was more sisterly than loverlike. Frances said gently, "Thanks, young one. Take care of yourself."

"I'll see you around."

Was she disappointed, or was this more or less what she had expected? Frances drove home with her eye on the rush-hour traffic and her mind on the afternoon's adventure. I always thought people who played around probably had a thin time of it, she mused. More anticipation than satisfaction. Different faces, different bodies, same gymnastics. Henry the Eighth

and Anne Boleyn. You can have an orgasm with just about anybody, and it may not mean a thing.

In a way, she wasn't sorry she had gone to the motel. She
was rid now of the curiosity, the desire that had tugged at her
mind and body ever since the girl had made her first approach.
It had been an interesting experience , and now she was free.
You don't know until you try — how many times had she heard
that? Having tried, she probably wasn't going through it again.
Not unless something unheard-of came into her life. A gorgeous
woman who would make love standing on her head or swinging on the chandelier, she thought with a totally unexpected
laugh.

According to the beliefs that had been planted in her in
childhood, she should have felt deeply guilty. Even if she were
so lost to her parents' ideas that she had become a lesbian —
more, had recognized and admitted that she had always been
a lesbian — she felt rather tired and a little bored. Relieved,
more than anything. There was Erika, but she would sort out
her feelings about Erika later. I suppose recreational sex is something, she thought as the little blue Datsun turned into her own
driveway like a well-trained horse, but it isn't everything. These
kids have a lot to learn.

EIGHTEEN

They joined NOW as soon as they heard about it, mailing their dues to national headquarters and not sorry, realizing that there was no chapter in Waubonsie, or later in Tucson. Erika said, "I like to support a good cause, but I hate going to meetings." They did join a woman's group that announced itself as supporting social reform and grudged the time they spent on it. The meetings were mostly dedicated to reading the minutes and planning fund-raising events, talking about supporting peace as long as it didn't involve unilateral disarmament, and generally approving of democracy. By this time the war in Vietnam had spread into Laos and Cambodia. It was, Frances thought, like hearing someone read a menu without being given any actual food. She decided that staff meetings were all the boredom she needed, and they stopped going to meetings.

"They're all white middle-class elitists," Erika pointed out. "No Chicanos, no Blacks, no Indians. Not one person who looked gay."

"You don't look gay," Frances pointed out. Erika was wearing a ruffled blouse and her favorite silver-and-turquoise earrings.

"Of course not. We're still in the closet. So is almost everyone we know." For by this time they were collecting, very gradually and cautiously, a small circle of lesbian friends, mostly professional women, mostly interested in music and theater. It was a process of accretion: you made a friend, and then you met your friend's friends. Erika said, "What I meant was, I didn't see anyone who looked like a couple."

"Suppose it comes up as an issue? They're raising hell over lesbians in the New York NOW, trying to throw them out."

"We'll deal with it when it happens."

This reasonable approach didn't keep the questions from recurring. Neither did staying home from meetings. They dealt with it, as many other women were doing, by paying their dues and letting it go at that.

They couldn't ignore the issue. Other people kept bringing it up. Irene Romero, head librarian at their neighborhood branch, asked, "What would you do if it came up in a staff meeting? Speak out or sit tight?"

Frances thought it over, turning her coffee cup slowly. "I don't know. I really like my job—I can't imagine switching. I don't want to make speeches or stand on street corners and hand out leaflets. New York seems so far away—sort of like a foreign country, don't you think? It's a whole different lifestyle, a different mentality. All this rebellion is okay for the young ones, but I'm fifty-four and I'm no revolutionary."

"Same, for me, I guess," Erika said a little sadly. "We have gay teachers—everyone knows who they are, really, but as long as nothing is said, it doesn't exist. Verbalizing makes it real." She sighed. "Teaching is a vulnerable field, and the higher they go the harder they fall."

The subject came up again on Sunday evening, when Irene and Betty came over for an informal supper. Irene, a kindergarten teacher, said quietly. "It" comes sooner or later. Look what happened to Kate Millett."

"Look what happened to Betty Friedan." Betty said bitterly. "We all bought that book and read it, we all believed it, we thought she meant it. The greatest thing since Kleenex. Now it turns out she doesn't want us in her fucking movement. We're the Lavender Menace. A whole section of the *New York Times*, stuffy old establishment paper."

"She's a middle-class housewife. She doesn't know any better."

"How's she going to learn if she won't listen? You'd think being gay was catching."

Frances suggested, "Probably she's never made love with anything but men, so she doesn't know anything about real fulfillment."

Erika said quietly, "We'll never get anywhere if we don't come out, and if we do we're discredited. Not to mention unemployed and hungry."

"Back to square one." Frances bit into a cookie. "I'll think about it tomorrow."

"That didn't work very well for Scarlett, either."

Later, in the middle of the night, Erika awoke, listened, and reached to touch Frances' shoulder. "You're not asleep."

Frances said dreamily, "It seems too bad when we have so much to give them."

There was no need for questions. "Sure. But we came to it the hard way. It took a long time. Some of us gave up our parents, husbands, even children — that's the hard one. It took a while to work it out for ourselves. Now we don't have to placate some man if we want to go to a meeting or sign a petition. Straight women really believe all that male superiority stuff, they've internalized the male values just as their mothers did. So they have to do it for themselves."

"I don't want to be a martyr. I like my job. But I have to live with myself. If there's a big change coming for women, how do we not get involved?"

"I've paid my dues." Erika closed her eyes against that old pain. A little girl coming home to find her mother and father and brother sprawled grotesquely across the ice-covered sidewalk, frozen into their own blood. What starts injustice? How do you prevent it, how do you heal those wounds?

She threw an arm across Frances, and after a little while felt her sigh and relax.

Carol had stopped being a pest after the motel incident. Perhaps she too had expected something new and exciting, something her young friends hadn't discovered. She and Frances passed in the halls with a casual, friendly greeting. Now she took to dropping in at the PT office when no one else was around. Which fortunately wasn't often. "Who's Rita Mae Brown?"

Frances searched her memory. "I think she used to write for the Ladder. Belongs to DOB, I think."

"What's DOB?"

"My God, don't you kids know anything about your own history? I thought you were a red-hot lesbian feminist. Next thing you'll be telling me you never heard of Susan B. Anthony."

"Is she that woman that ran for Congress back east?"

"I give up. Don't you ever read anything?"

"I don't have time to read."

"That's like not having time to breathe. Where did you hear about Rita Mae Brown?"

"She resigned from NOW, whatever that is. All those letters; it's worse than the government."

"National Organization for Women. Aren't you interested at all in what happens to women? Getting equal pay, getting to work at whatever they want?"

"Only my sisters." Carol said cheerfully. "I don't give a good goddam what happens to straight women. That's their problem."

"I suppose you don't give a damn what happens to men and children, either."

"Men are the enemy. I don't know any children."

"That's heterosexual thinking," Frances said firmly. "Me and my wife and my son John and his wife."

Carol looked puzzled. "It's an old saying," Frances explained. "Why did she resign?"

"Who? Oh, Rita whatserface. Because they wouldn't put gay rights in their platform, or something. She says we have to organize something of our own. I'm in favor of that."

"As long as someone else does the organizing. Scram, I'm busy."

This dialogue, reported at the supper table, got a wry smile from Erika. "What's this kid doing for her sisters she's so concerned about?"

"Going to bed with as many of them as possible. I suppose that's a form of social action. Any time Carol's late for work, you can bet she has a new relationship going."

Erika looked at her, but Frances looked away. Erika, with her sensitivity to inflections and facial expressions, suspected that something involving Carol had happened or was happening or was on the verge of happening, but she repressed all desire to pry. If Frances felt guilty or uneasy, she would have to deal with it in her own way and at her own time. She said quietly, "Don't put the kid down. She may be a little half-baked, but every revolution has some of those. Some of them are brave, and some are smart enough to learn."

Frances said, "Sometimes I wish we lived in New York or on the West Coast, where things are happening. They've organized something called Radicalesbians, for political action. If we lived in San Francisco we could take part in things and still keep our personal life to ourselves, I think. Or we could get jobs with gay groups."

"I have a feeling it's not that simple. And there may be enough action here to keep you happy. This thing is growing."

Frances sighed. "I think I'm getting old. I'd like everything to stay the way it was, and at the same time I'd like things to get better. It makes me nervous."

"I missed my period this month," Erika said. "You can hold my hand when I start getting hot flashes. Let's get old together and let the kids worry about the future."

NINETEEN

The poster in the front window said McGOVERN EAGLE-TON. When people pointed out that Eagleton was no longer in the running, Erika said it was insane to bar a man from public office because he had sense enough to go to the doctor when he was sick—who were the crazies anyhow? "Might as well put him down for going to the dentist when he has a toothache." She washed carefully around the poster. "I do hate washing windows."

"Why don't we hire someone to do the work?"

"Costs too much. Anyway they don't do it right. If we're going to buy a house, we need to save every nickel."

Frances, running the vacuum, brushed a wisp of hair off her nose with the back of her hand. "I don't see why. We're paying two hundred, plus utilities, and it goes up June first. Monthly payments on a mortgage won't come to much more, and when it's paid for we have something to show for it."

"There's always a lot of small print in those contracts." Erika backed down off the stepladder. "A house of our own. I never thought I'd love to have one."

"Me neither."

"You had a house in Waubonsie, with a garbage disposal and electric dishwasher and two bathrooms."

"That was Bill's. I was allowed to live there because I was a Mrs."

"Do you want to look at some more places this afternoon?"

Frances considered. "I don't think so. I'm still feeling queasy."

"It's that damn cafeteria."

"I don't think so. More like I'm coming down with the flu. So all right, let's get done here and go see what the agency has lined up for us. I'm holding out for a yard, though."

"Thank God for casual dressing." In the middle west, house-hunting would have called for skirts, hose, heels. Erika ran a comb through her hair, put on a clean shirt and came out to join Frances. "You really do feel a bit rocky, don't you?"

"Do me good to get out."

Erika laid the back of a slightly damp hand on Frances' forehead. "Mmm, you might be a little bit feverish. Why don't you stay home and take some aspirin?"

"I'm all right."

It was April, as hot as July in Illinois but with an ineffable spring sweetness in the air. The tangle of bushes beside the back door was studded with small purple blossoms; three or four honeybees buzzed around it. "Do you suppose that's bee balm? I keep meaning to look it up at the library. The pictures in the nature books never look like the real plants."

Erika consulted the realty companies list. "Here's one close by, and a woman runs it."

The woman was small, artificially blonde, heavily made up and hung about with silver and turquoise jewelry. "You're a teacher, Miss Frohmann? Oh, a principal. My, that's very nice. What does your husband do?"

"I'm single."

"Oh, and you brought a friend to look at the house. Well, two heads are always better than one. Mrs. — Miss — "

"Kirby. We're planning to buy a house together."

The change in expression was instant and complete, as though someone had pulled a mask over the smooth smiling face. She had been through this before, regretted the necessity, but had a polite little canned speech that would save everyone embarrassment. "We really prefer to sell to young couples, or retired people — most of them have a little nest egg and that does make things so much easier, doesn't it? However, if one of you has a brother or son who would sign the lease, someone responsible — "

Erika said icily, "We are both quite responsible. Professional people."

"I'm sorry, I'm sure you are. It's just company policy."

Frances said, "That's illegal and you know it. Why should you discriminate against us because we're women?"

"I don't, I really don't. If it were my decision I'd be glad to sell you a house, company policy—"

Erika asked, "Why do you work for a company that discriminates against women?"

"I can't see that it's any of your business."

Erika turned to go, then turned back. "You realize that we're reporting you to the Better Business Bureau." She walked grandly to the car, trailed by Frances.

"I wonder if there's a gay realtor in this town? Must be. Or how we'd find him, or her, or them." She waited for Frances to climb in beside her. "Fran, you really are sick." For Frances had doubled up and was retching miserably, holding the door handle.

"Something I ate."

"Like hell! Get in here. We're going to the hospital."

Erika had not been in a hospital for twenty years. She had forgotten the long waits, the impersonal attitudes of doctors and nurses, the forms that had to be filled out. She supposed that Frances took all this for granted. She worked every day in this atmosphere of not-quite-kindness. At any rate, she looked too sick to care. "They can get my records from the clinic," she said thickly. "Birthmarks and all. "You wait here while they poke at me."

"You know what it is, don't you?" A fat, white-haired doctor had come into the emergency room and was looking at her with a smile, as if this were a social call. Frances looked at him with relief. "One gets you ten it's my appendix," she told him.

"I never bet on a sure thing. Get her on the cart and roll her into x-ray. This your roommate, Fran? Let her fill out the goddam forms. You haven't got a lot of time to lose."

Frances told Erika. "Don't look like that. An appendix is nothing. It won't even cost us anything—fringe benefits. Hang around." They lifted her onto the gurney and she was silent, as if talking were too much effort. Erika looked after her as the orderly trundled her down the hall.

A nurse brought Erika a cup of coffee. "Having an appendix out these days is nothing," she said cheerfully. "You can stay till she's out of the recovery room. You don't know me, but she got my sister's kid off crutches and back on his feet a couple years ago."

The waiting room was more cheerful than the ones at the clinic, with yellow walls, orange curtains, and potted cacti. A young man sat in one corner, staring gloomily into space. Prospective father, Erika thought, wishing he hadn't been so horny and promising himself it won't happen again. Lots of luck, bud.

She looked away from him and found herself praying, to whom or what she didn't know. It seemed obvious that God, if one existed, was male and supremely indifferent to the little problems of human beings. A female deity would have designed the human body more efficiently, leaving out germ traps like appendices, tonsils, and gall bladders, not to mention taking the muss and fuss out of the female reproductive system. Still, she found herself saying *Please let her be all right, I'll never ask for anything again, I know it's a simple routine operation, they do it all the time, but anyhow.* Peritonitis. Why did we wait so long?

The young man asked in a hoarse voice, "What's wrong with your patient?"

"Appendicitis. It's pretty routine. I think."

"They're working on my girlfriend in there. We were in a motorcycle accident." He was very young, not more than twenty. "Some asshole ran the red light and didn't even slow down. We don't have any money, no insurance or anything."

"Is she badly hurt?"

"Her pelvis might be broken. And concussion. Is that bad?"

"Concussion? I don't think so. They see double for a while, or dizzy, or something. Are you all right?" His cheek was scratched and discolored, his shirt torn.

"Why couldn't it have been me? Why did it have to be her? She might be pregnant, too. She's been worrying about it. She's afraid to tell her folks, if she is."

"Well," Erika said grimly, "that's one thing she won't have

to worry about any more, if her pelvis is broken. They'll take care of it, if the accident didn't. Her folks will never know."

"I wouldn't mind. I'd kind of like a kid, you know what I mean?" He was looking at her for reassurance — a grownup whose hair had begun to gray. She said, "It's a good hospital, she'll be all right."

She fell into a half-sleep and found herself in Steinhagen. She hadn't thought about Steinhagen, consciously, for a long time. The nightmares that had haunted her in the resettlement camp and in her first years in America had faded away, were washed out by time. Now she was in Steinhagen, waiting for morning inspection, and someone was screaming. She woke, sweating, and found herself in the yellow and orange waiting room, the outdoor light fading beyond the windows. Someone *was* screaming, but far away. There were quick footsteps and then silence. Her throat was dry. She asked the boy, "Is there any place where I can get a cup of coffee?"

She reached for her purse. He said, "Here, let me." She recognized an act of propitiation, and nodded. "Thank you, that would be nice of you."

A sturdy candy-striper came to the door. "Are you Erika? My name's Carol. I work with Frances. I thought I'd hang around a while, maybe till she's out of surgery."

"How long will she be in the hospital, do you know?"

"Depends. She's a real good lady, you know? Anyway she's covered for care. We all are, all the clinic employees."

Erika looked at Carol and saw a middle-sized young woman with shiny dark hair, neither pretty nor ugly, neither tall nor short. Average. I don't give a damn what's happened between her and Fran, Erika thought. She's a sister and it was good of her to come here. She put a hand on Carol's shoulder. "She'll be all right, I think."

"Oh sure. She may look kind of green — that's the anesthetic, don't let that throw you."

Young Mr. Sanders came back with two plastic cups, generously handed his own to Carol, and jumped as a nurse looked in. "You can come in now, Mr. Sanders, but don't stay long. She's pretty woozy."

I hope it's good news, Erika thought. I hope his girl will be all right. I hope she wasn't pregnant. These straight people really have problems.

I hope things work out all right for the whole poor damn dumb human race. They won't, of course, but somebody has to have a little good luck once in a while. Let Frances be all right, let the kid's girl be all right.

Carol gave her a sharp look. "I hope you know how lucky you are."

Erika swallowed. "Yes, I know. It's good to have a sister here at a time like this."

"Sure." Carol picked up a magazine, riffled through the pages and put it down again. "When she comes to, give her my love and tell her I'll see her tomorrow, after work."

Erika nodded.

TWENTY

As often happens, the house they finally found was not exactly what they were looking for. Nor was it luxurious according to Sun Belt standards—no swimming pool—and it was located conveniently close to a supermarket, bank, and drugstore instead of elegantly secluded in the foothills. The patio was a strip of sand studded with tufts of bermuda grass, and there were not enough closets. But there was a spreading mulberry tree in the back yard, with small gray lizards running around its scaly gray bark on hot days, and the building itself was adobe with a roof of terra cotta tiles. Best of all, there was a dining room—not a corner of the kitchen nor an end of the living room, but an actual dining room with space for an extension table, six chairs, and a small credenza. Erika said, "It will be so wonderful to eat without moving papers off the table." She hadn't mentioned it before, but now she sounded as if she had been deprived of the amenities for a long time.

What really closed the sale was the attitude of the realtor, a tall, husky young man with a bushy, black beard; he seemed more interested in their credit rating than in their sexual orientation. The payments were more than they had budgeted—about a hundred dollars a month more. "But everything's going up. If we wait till next year, the interest rates may be higher. We won't buy anything." They signed the papers after a preliminary reading by their own lawyer—among their slowly, cautiously growing Sunday-supper group was a determined young lesbian out to make a name for herself as a defense attorney—and went home to wait. "I'm ready to start packing," Frances said. "Let's hope it's settled before the Christmas holidays set in."

November came. They went to the neighborhood schoolhouse to cast their vote. Richard Nixon was elected in spite of

115

them. "They asked for it." Frances said dejectedly. "The fools deserve whatever they get." What they were to get would be Watergate, but no one could see that far ahead.

Television talk shows echoed with predictions. Laos and Cambodia fell before American know-how and superior weaponry. The government had pledged to stay out of those countries. Now there were newspaper admissions of Napalm and Agent Orange, of fragmentation bombs released by the image on a radar screen two hundred miles away from the jungle path where something moved — perhaps a human being, perhaps a ground squirrel.

Erika cut a picture of the temples at Angkor Wat from an old *National Geographic* and tacked it to the bulletin board in her office. It seemed as remote in history as the Parthenon, as the ships at Salamis.

The National Organization of Women issued a belated manifesto: "Be it resolved that NOW recognizes the double oppression of lesbians." Frances said, "Sure, that'll have about as much effect as desegregating the schools." For the television screen showed white parents, their faces distorted with hate, screaming curses after the busloads of little black children on their way to first-grade classrooms. "It won't change anyone's feelings."

"Gives us a legal handle in specific cases."

In the east, the Radicalesbians were protesting, not the indignities forced on them by society but the determination of some women to regard their sons, brothers, and even husbands as human beings. Applying for divorce, they sued for custody of their little girls but renounced their sons. An organization called Redstockings sprang into being, and there was a sudden proliferation of magazines and newspapers crammed with coming-out stories and articles about what was and was not politically correct. Frances subscribed to everything. Small magazines in plain brown wrappers arrived, were glanced at and put aside. The movement was on its way. Where, no one was sure. In the meantime, opposition gathered strength, the word *homosexual* appeared in newspapers for the first time, and television evangelists began ranting against this titillating new sin.

They moved in January, with eight women and three pickup trucks to do the work. The man next door sauntered out into his driveway and watched. At first Frances thought that he had come to offer his help and was divided between accepting and politely rejecting it — after all, women were capable of lifting and carrying anything a man could handle. She might as well not have worried; after a few minutes he was joined by another middle-aged male, heavy-set and crew-cut. They watched for a few minutes. Then the first said, quite audibly, "Goddam dykes," and they went into the house next door. Barbara said cheerfully, "Goddam male chauvinist pigs."

"Ignore him. He's just an Archie Bunker."

Later, as they sat on the living room floor drinking beer and eating tacos, Barbara said, "I hope you two have a gun, in case you need it."

"Good God, no."

"Better get one. There's been a lot of robberies lately, anyhow."

Erika said firmly. "No way. People are always getting killed because some fool shoots before he thinks. The guy wakes up and hears a burglar, and it turns out to be his wife coming back from the bathroom."

"What'll you do if a robber breaks in?"

"Hit him with anything I can get my hands on. Bash him with a hammer or take a knife to him. I'm no pacifist." Erika thought it over. "Most likely I'd be too petrified to do anything."

"Look, the people on the other side are going somewhere." A rush to the uncurtained window, to see the fair-haired young man with the short haircut, the blonde young woman in designer jeans, and the two cute little tow-headed children piling into a station wagon. "Air Force," Phyllis decided. "They send all the blondes to the southwest, to make it clear who belongs to the master race. The dark-haired ones get assigned to Minnesota, or someplace."

"You're kidding."

"Maybe. You're in enemy country here though."

She was kidding — maybe — but it took Erika a few mornings of leaving for work before she stopped looking around, feeling relieved when none of the neighbors were in sight. "I feel like the first black family to move into a white neighborhood," she admitted. Frances said, "Hah, nobody's burned any crosses on our lawn, have they?"

"Not yet. Does the Klan hate gays?"

"The Klan hates everybody but rednecks."

"In that case I'm going to feel insulted if they don't do anything. It's like being left off McCarthy's list."

"The neighbors probably have things of their own to attend to."

Moving felt like a turning point in their life together. They looked at themselves and their daily routines much as they looked at their furniture, exposed to the unflattering light of day. Erika was thinner than ever but said she felt fine. Her theory was that there are two kinds of women, those who get thin as they age and those who get fat. The gray threads were multiplying In her short fair hair and she refused to have it tinted; it was stupid, she said, in a climate where she had to shampoo every day. The fine lines at the corners of her eyes were hidden by her fashionably large glasses. Teachers were supposed to wear glasses, anyhow. To Frances she looked more than ever like a little fair-haired boy. Frances, nine years older, felt a pang when she took this birdlike being into her arms.

Frances was gaining a little weight, had developed high blood pressure, which put both of them on a low-salt diet, and said gloomily that she dreaded old age. "That's because so many of your patients are old. You don't see the eighty-year-olds out on the golf course and taking aerobics."

The goings-on in Vietnam, never to be recognized officially as war, stumbled to a close. The newspaper accounts held a terrible fascination for Erika, survivor of Steinhagen. "They have bombs filled with metal barbs that tear people's insides into rags. Bombs full of plastic bits that don't show up on an X-ray screen. Probably germ warfare—where else can all this flu come from?" She brooded, propping her chin on her thin hand. "Don't people ever learn?"

"Darling, I wish you wouldn't read the papers."

Erika's smile glittered and vanished. "I wish so too. There isn't any answer, except doing what we can. It's so little."

Then, suddenly, quietly, it was over."

"Thousands dead, hundreds missing. They're shipping the bodies home in plastic bags. I thought the Nazis were the last of the barbarians."

Frances said, "Remember the newsreels of the old wars? The ticker-tape parades, and girls kissing the heroes? These kids coming back are being yelled at and called murderers. They look sort of sad and surprised."

"Well, the best were in Canada and Sweden — and in jail."

"The ones who fought didn't know any better. Not till it was too late."

Erika was implacable. "They knew it, they didn't let themselves know it, but they really did. We weren't saving the world for democracy or getting rid of Hitler, we were killing babies, bombing hospitals. Calling it a war on communism." Erika stopped to search out her thoughts. "In the Middle Ages, if you didn't like somebody you called him a heretic. Now he's a communist. Doesn't mean anything."

"Barb's brother is home. On hard drugs, zonked out of his skull, living from one needle to the next."

"Of course, how else could they stand it?"

There was a furious newspaper battle over amnesty. The young men in Canada and Sweden wanted to come home. Their families wanted them home. Couldn't they be pardoned?

"For what, for being right?"

"The people who were wrong can't forgive these guys for being right. That's why they're making all the fuss about the MIA's."

"I doubt," Erika said sadly, "that the human race is capable of ever learning anything."

The beefy man next door had an American flag on his porch, even when it rained, and a bumper sticker, FIND THE MIA'S, on his car. They heard him talking to his friends, barbecuing steaks in the side yard. "Well, the commies have won. We better get organized before they take over this country too." As far as Erika and Frances could see, the only organizing he did was

adding a National Rifle Association sticker to the collection
on the back of his car. They retaliated with a Women Strike for
Peace sticker. Frances asked. "Should we have one made up
'Dykes of the World Unite'?"

"Let's not get competitive. That's a male reaction."

"I'm willing to be ignored."

Just the same, when women arrived singly and in pairs for
Sunday-night supper, they felt a little nervous about Mr.
Marcussen's probable reaction. (There was a Mrs. Marcussen
who spent a great deal of time watering the lawn on their side,
but never spoke.)

As people do, they had gathered a group of friends, women
with similar interests and enough differences to make conversation stimulating: a nurse and a middle-aged doctor who had
lived together for fifteen years, a dreamy young woman who
worked in the downtown library in the daytime and painted
at night, and in 1973, Kim Vecchio. She and Frances had met
in a bookstore, which seemed like a good omen.

Kim lived in her van, which she parked in the yard of any
friend who was willing to have it. She had dropped out of college to work as a stage manager, but quit when she found that
her predecessor, a man, had been getting exactly twice what
she was getting. From somewhere she had scraped together
enough money to rent a small, dim room in the rundown area
still called downtown, now a place of gaping storefronts and
uneasy panhandlers, and was trying to start a feminist bookstore. There were feminist books now (always had been, Erika
pointed out — what about Mary Wollstonecraft?) but their pub-
lishers were operating on a thin shoestring and were not eager
to let unknown merchandisers have books on consignment. Most
of her sales were of the small magazines that appeared and
disappeared; Erika said they would be valuable someday, like
the early issues of *Poetry*. She wore grubby jeans and thrift
shop shirts, passionately defended any unpopular cause she
could get a handle on, and loved arguing.

Frances worried. "I don't know what she lives on."

"Ideals and raw vegetables, like all those kids."

"Ask her for Sunday night. I'll make something with cheese in it."

On Sunday night she showed up with a handful of garden flowers which Frances hoped she hadn't picked en route, and plans for a theatrical experiment. "Definitely off-Broadway, whatever Broadway is here." She had been talking with women on campus—she was auditing a course in Romance languages —and they were interested. "A couple of them have plays they've written. All we need is a little money and a lot of volunteers."

There was a small silence. Erika asked, "Lesbian plays?"

"One is and one isn't. We'll have to get word out to the women's community."

Erika reflected silently that there wasn't any such thing. It would have solved a lot of problems if there had been— and created a lot more, most likely. When you said women's community you meant lesbians, and they were fragmented too.

She picked up the sandwich platter and carried it into the kitchen. It was her experience that debate bred hunger; people ate without realizing it, lost in ideas.

It was evident that experimental theater wasn't going to get much help from straight women. Would she and Frances be brave enough, or foolhardy enough, to get involved in one of Kim's projects?

She had come to terms with her own sexuality at seventeen, when she left her American foster home and moved in with Martha Weber—dear Martha, part teacher and part lover and, she admitted it now, part mother. Martha had been reluctant to be the lover of a pupil, but that relationship had washed away any guilt Erika might have felt. How can you be guilty when you feel so fulfilled?

But she was guilty of being silent when people repeated stupid jokes about queers, when she heard some psychological nonsense about the grimness and frustration of lesbian life. As though there were no lonely spinsters and widows, no unhappy wives! Magazines and television networks were beginning to touch timidly on the subject, recruiting "experts" in a clumsy but no doubt sincere desire to show all sides. She and Frances watched them hopefully and saw that they weren't uncovering any new facts or reaching the enemy — the queer-haters.

I'm simply not political, Erika thought, carrying a new stack of sandwiches back to the living room. I don't want to be classified. I really don't mind working with men as long as they keep their hands off me — a problem that shrinks as one ages. Age does have its compensations.

Kim asked, "Will you help? We need everything, stage hands, everything."

A married look passed between Frances and Erika. Frances said. "I'm willing to type parts and help with rehearsals — you'll have to rehearse evenings, won't you? It's time we did something besides go to work and come home again."

"Erika?"

"If you can find something that doesn't involve publicity," Erika said. Then, "Okay. I'm willing."

TWENTY-ONE

"A little to the left."

"Shift 'er about two inches."

Frances lugged the table into place and wiped her face on a grimy shirtsleeve. "That about right?"

"Bets, does that give you clearance for your entrance? Try it. Okay, everybody, thanks a lot, a good dress rehearsal, and don't you believe that means a bad performance, there's nothing in it. I'll see you here tomorrow night, one hour before curtain time. Advance sales on tickets have been pretty good."

It should be, Frances thought. Everyone connected with the production of *Time Enough* had been peddling tickets, and those with jobs had invested as heavily as they could. She had bought half a dozen and passed them out at work, mostly to Carol and her friends who didn't have five dollars to spare but could be counted on for enthusiastic applause. "At this rate we can't afford to be patrons of the arts," she complained to Erika. "We'll be eating beans for a week, and my sacroiliac will never be the same again."

"It will be interesting to see if we get any press coverage."

"If we do, they won't even mention that it's a play about lesbians."

"They might not realize it. It's more like an attack on marriage—like George Bernard Shaw or something." Erika, having done the typing and editing early on, was free of further responsibility and had beer sitting in the back of the room, where she tested for audibility.

"You don't think it's a good play."

"I didn't say that. It's allegorical, and some people may not get the deeper meaning. You could say the same thing about *Waiting for Godot*."

"Anyhow, all we can do is hope for the best."

Kim trailed up to them as they stood beside the curb. "All we can do tonight. Some of us are going over to Earth Goddess for something to eat — want to come along?"

They consulted each other with a look. "Shall we? I'd rather have a hamburger," Erika said. "Thanks, but Fran has a backache. Tomorrow's a hard day for both of us. We'll run you over there, though."

"No need. Thanks a lot, you've both been great."

She didn't thank anyone else. "That means we are still outsiders," Erika pointed out as they got into the car. "The question is, are we getting the respectful treatment because we're old or because we have steady jobs?"

"It's a nice change. I'm used to being put down for being old and respected for being solvent."

"Do you think Tucson is ready for this kind of drama?"

"Was Athens ready for Euripides? Not that this kid is batting in the same league."

"Come on, it's not a bad play. There ought to be someone around who'll like it. I love every semicolon in the damn thing, having stayed up half the night typing, but I doubt it will go down in history. Most things don't. I quoted something from de la Mare to an English teacher the other day," Erika said sadly, "and she said, 'who's she?' "

The little blue Datsun was waiting in front of Walgreen's, almost the only car on the block. Downtown closed at five o'clock. Frances unlocked the door. "Judy and Helen were held up last week. Kid walked up to the car as they were pulling out of an outdoor parking lot — of all places — and took their pocketbooks at knife-point. It's getting so we have all the modern conveniences, just like Chicago and L.A."

"In Chicago or L.A., they'd have been stabbed. I don't like the idea, but maybe we ought to have a gun."

"This from you! I wouldn't say no to a Mace spray, but they don't seem to advertise them anymore. Probably hit myself in the eye with it."

The familiar streets slipped past, houses showing the ghostly blue light of television screens, teenagers hanging out at

McDonald's and Jack in the Box, a single jogger putting in his mileage under the feeble glow of the street lamps, people filling their gas tanks at the self-serve stations. "This town still looks like a village. I hope it stays that way for a long time, though we could use some street lights."

"They keep it dim for the observatory. Too many lights make the sky harder to read."

"They don't care how many people get mugged and raped?"

Mr. Marcussen was washing his car under a brilliant yardlight when they drove in. Mrs. Marcussen was watching him. They looked up, but made no sign of recognition. The Air Force couple on the other side were sitting around their patio with half a dozen friends, around the debris of a barbecue. "Wondering what sort of an orgy we've been to," Frances said sourly as they unlocked the back door. The breakfast dishes were still on the kitchen table. "I don't mind staying out late and being tired the next day, but I do hate coming home to a messy house."

"I could use a sandwich. Have we got any makings?"

"Cheese or peanut butter or egg."

"Cheese, toasted." Erika whisked the dried-on plates into the sink, then sat down beside the table and unrolled the morning paper. "More hoohah about the MIAs. Hasn't it occurred to anybody that some of those boys want to stay there? They're married to Vietnamese girls and living on those little rice farms. I wouldn't want to come home, in their place."

Frances ran water into the percolator and slid the sandwiches in the oven. "Hottest night in the year, why are we doing this . . . what's the matter?" Erika had dropped the paper and was looking at her strangely. "I'm sorry I'm a fussy old lady."

"It's not that," Erika said as she held up the paper in her hand.

The sheet Erika held out was headed MONEY. Frances said, "What on earth?" They had no investments, the house payments ate up all the money they could spare. Then she saw the photograph—small but clear—and snatched the sheet from Erika's hands.

"Plastix Produx, Inc. is announcing the transfer to its new Phoenix plant of Robert W. Ollenfield, former Vice-President in Charge of Sales, located for the past three years in the company's Albuquerque office. Ollenfield is the son of company head William Ollenfield, who started Plastix Produx in 1944 and developed it into a multi-million-dollar concern. Mrs. Ollenfield, the former Mari Kerner, is well known in Albuquerque circles as a patroness of music and theater. They will move to Phoenix in the near future. Welcome to Arizona's expanding business community."

"I'll be damned. Bob and Mari in Arizona."

Erika folded the paper and laid it on the drainboard. "We never go to Phoenix. I haven't been there since last year's teachers' convention. We're no more likely to see him than when he lived in Chicago — or Albuquerque."

"Or Waubonsie," Frances said with an attempt at a smile. "I'm not going to be upset, honestly I'm not. Just came as a surprise, that's all." Frances found a crumpled tissue in her shirt pocket and blew her nose. "I must be getting senile or something. I don't give a damn about Bill. I don't hate him, I don't want to see him. It's as if he never existed, but Bob — all these years I've trained myself not to think about him. But I did give birth to that kid, I do remember how he was when he was a little boy. I never felt very close to him. He was a self-contained sort of kid. His father wanted him to be macho — you know, real men don't cry. I knew I wouldn't see much of him after he married Mari. But Erika, wouldn't you think he would have wondered about me once in a while? Just wondered if I were alive?"

"Maybe he did. Mari — "

"Mari, hell. What is he, a man or a mouse?"

"From what you've told me about her, anybody who marries that one is going to be a mouse."

"A nice, hard-working money-producing mouse."

"Suppose he felt as bad as you do, would that make you feel any happier?"

Frances poured a cup of coffee and splashed milk into it

from the waxed carton. Her hand was shaking. "I know I'm being foolish. I'm just tired."

"You're being human. If I had a child—if I had a third cousin alive I'd try to get in touch. I never see the name Frohmann without wondering, and the New York phone book is full of Frohmanns. That's dumb but normal."

"I suppose he hates me." Coffee splashed from the cup onto Frances' already crumpled and soiled shirt front. "His father and Mari, that polite bitch, they'll have seen to that."

"I know." Erika gave up all thought of getting any coffee herself; she yanked the oven door open and took out the cookie sheet with the slightly scorched sandwiches. She put her hands on Frances' shoulder and pushed her into a chair. "Now you listen to me. You don't know what Bob thinks about you, or *if* he thinks about you, or if he's ever tried to find you. You never let him know where you were, did you? You could have called him up at his office, or written him a letter—you didn't want any contact with him. Okay?"

"I like my life," Frances told her, taking a sandwich and looking at it doubtfully. "I'd rather be with you than with anyone else in the world. I wouldn't have gone on the way I was."

Erika laid a gray-streaked head against her shoulder. "Frannie, do you know how many women have made that choice? Young girls whose parents have thrown them out. How do you think they survived? Women whose husbands have taken their children away from them. Bob was an adult, he was on the edge of getting married when you left. That's part of the lesbian experience, part of coming out. That's why we have to depend on one another. We're all the family there is."

"I'm not complaining."

"What would you talk about if you ran into Bob somewhere? The weather? Look, you have to get through this by yourself. Are those sandwiches fit to eat?"

"If you don't mind a little charcoal. Good for the teeth."

Erika tore the newsprint sheet in fourths and stuffed them into the wastebasket. "Just so you don't start sniffling all over again. Why don't we go to bed. It's after midnight."

"That's the best idea you've had all day."

She showered sketchily, climbed into their double bed, and shook her head at the pill Erika offered. "I don't approve of sleeping pills."

"I don't either. That's why they work so well when we take them." Erika gathered her close. For a while after Frances' breathing slowed and smoothed, her lover lay awake in the summer darkness. What she saw there kept her awake, tired as she was.

Finally, her arm asleep, she shifted Frances' weight to the other side of the bed and tiptoed into the bathroom, shook another pill from the bottle and gulped it down. Picking her way back to the bed, she stopped to look out of the window.

The neighborhood was quiet. The Air Force people had gone home. The Marcussen's yapping little dog had gone to sleep, and the houses on both sides were dark. A car turned at the corner and faded into silence. The moon was sinking, but there was enough light to define the cacti they had planted in the patio, the thick leaves of the mulberry tree stirring silently in the late-night breeze. Beyond was the city, the hum of the police helicopter keeping watch over the sleepers.

It seemed infinitely peaceful. And precious.

She got back into bed and settled down with an arm across Frances, who was not only asleep but snoring a little. So much for romance, Erika thought drowsily. All right, real life is better. She turned so that their feet touched, and fell asleep.

TWENTY-TWO

The city was growing. It had always attracted tourists, from the days when the lungers camped out in the desert, trying to bake the tuberculosis bacilli out of their bodies under the dazzling sun. In the depression, families tractored out of their homes in the Dust Bowl moved in, not in the numbers that invaded California but enough to create problems for the new welfare system. Mexicans, legal and otherwise, came and went. And with the arrival of Social Security, a whole generation of old people headed for the Sun Belt, many arriving in Arizona where the winters were warmer than in Florida and the summers were dryer than in California. Real estate operators, resort managers, and supermarket chains thrived on the influx. Old residents complained about the rising crime rate. Local industries, non-union and low-pay for the most part, found themselves with a bigger labor pool than they needed. Tucson still looked like an overgrown village — vacant lots studded with cacti — but it was becoming a metropolis.

Erika said dryly, "We're like the people who live by taking in each other's washing — we sell each other houses and lots. At least it's one field where women get paid the same as men."

"Good for my business." Frances reminded her, "You can't walk down the street without falling over little old ladies. Good for people who sell canes, crutches, and walkers too. It's going to be another Miami by the time we retire, God forbid."

"What have you got against little old ladies?"

"Not a thing. They're some of my nicest patients."

"Then you have something against Miami?"

"Not a thing. I just prefer saguaros to rhinestones."

"You may see this town as a senior citizens' paradise," Erika concluded, "but the school system is getting bigger every

year, and the birthrate is down. The kids have to be coming
from somewhere."

"Over the border?"

"Over several borders. We're getting a lot of Orientals—
refugees. More Native American families are sending their kids
to school. I can cope with elementary Spanish, but it's Vietnamese and Korean and Yaqui and Papago—excuse me,
O'odham. They're nice kids, though. And smart."

"Now you're getting bilingual classrooms, you'll have to
start working more." Erika's struggle to keep Spanish in the
classroom had put her on the front page more than once, as a
feisty fighter for what the Anglos saw as expensive frills and
the Hispanic parents regarded as recognition of their culture.
Pictures of her, small and gently smiling, confused those who
wanted to think of her as a flaming crusader, some kind of
radical. Barbara asked. "How do you communicate?"

"Pats and smiles. The other kids are my best help, they
teach without knowing it. My little new Koreans are speaking
a wonderful mishmash of English and Spanish."

Downtown, the heart of the city before World War I, was
beginning to disintegrate. Businesses moved to the outlying shopping plazas with their covered walls and huge parking lots.
Tucsonans were drivers, not walkers: almost the only people
you saw on the sidewalk were rigged out in jogging clothes.
Now they could drive to a shopping mall, visit a dozen stores,
have lunch and see a movie without walking more than a few
steps. Like Springfield, Illinois, Springfield, Missouri, and Springfield, Massachusetts, Tucson was becoming less a city than a
string of shopping centers.

"But why do they cover the walkways, in this climate?"

"To keep us cool. Or because that's the way they did it and
nobody ever questioned it. Like Howard Johnson and Trail-
ways and McDonald's. They're all alike, except here they have
cactus." Three or four established department stores quietly
left downtown and moved to the malls. Around the bus stations there grew up a network of cheap rooming houses, adult
bookstores, and thrift shops. A hopeful developer built a maze
of small high-priced specialty shops near the postoffice and

courthouses — two-story buildings, the extra story being underground, reached by elevators. There were no sign posts, and
Barbara insisted that she had been lost for half a day, trying to
keep an appointment at a sandwich shop. These tourist-
directed places were given romantic Spanish names in the time-
honored tradition of celebrating the storied past and ignoring
history. Frances said angrily, "As if the Hispanics weren't always low man on the totem pole."

"No, love, that's the Indians."

"I'd like to get more Papago kids into the system." Erika's
forehead creased. "They're sent out of state to boarding schools
and de-Indianized."

Frances said, "I never thought I'd find myself married to
a crusader."

"Being an Indian in the southwest is like being a Jew in
Austria, in 1939."

There was a small silence. Then Frances said, determinedly
cheerful, "I had the strangest dream the other night. I dreamed
I was on top of Kitt Peak, dusting the mountain with a feather
duster."

"Dusting the observatory?"

"It wasn't there, nor anything else. But the funny thing
was, I went up inside the mountain, in an elevator."

"Getting it ready for the tourists? Beats walking up."

Frances glared, then grinned. "I'm surprised the Chamber
of Commerce hasn't thought of it."

"Yeh, the C of C is great on reconstructing the past — as
long as they don't have to do without electricity and running
water."

Frances, there for supper and lingering to talk, said, "What
they need is a woman on the council. A black lesbian, like the
story about the man who saw God."

City or not, there were still no street lights on their block,
and no sidewalk in front of their house. The new houses had
little strips of concrete in front of them awaiting the day when
they would be joined with others, but everyone rode — cars,
vans, trucks, bicycles, motorcycles, skateboards. Traffic was a

tangle despite the lights. It was a holdover from pioneer days that they didn't much care for.

Kim's little theater went broke and Kim drifted on, not to be heard from again. The town now had a sizable community of young women in jeans and sandals, or long skirts, who moved in and out of small shops where they sold herbs, or candles, or leather goods, or hand-crafted pottery, or jewelry, or Tarot cards and copies of the *I Ching*. On her days off Frances liked to drift into these places and get acquainted, sometimes make a small purchase. Sometimes she met with aloofness or impersonal courtesy, inspired by her age or her middle-class look. Sometimes a friendship developed and the young craftswoman joined the Sunday-night supper group. There was a casual acceptance among these women that she could have used at their age, a rejection of lifestyles that didn't suit them, as though they were not worth bothering about.

Some were lesbians and said so, some at the first meeting. They weren't militant, like the women in the desert commune —they went their way and let others go theirs. Perhaps that was better than the old way of anger and rebellion. But how, Frances wondered, did you reach the women who hadn't found their own pattern?

She said to Erika, "They're so cool. I envy that. But how do they connect?"

"Maybe they don't want to connect."

"If that's the wave of the future, I'd just as soon not be here to see it."

"How old is this Hallie?" The latest discovery, a weaver of wall hangings.

"Thirty, maybe. They're all kids. Maybe she could come to supper Sunday night."

Hallie was surprised at the invitation, but willing to try anything once. "Only I'm a vegetarian, you know."

"We'll have an omelet." Frances hesitated. "Is there anyone you'd like to bring?"

"Not really. I don't have any special lover. In fact, I'm into celibacy right now."

This was as astonishing as group sex had been a few years earlier. "On a long-term basis?"

"I'm going to try it for a year. A lot of people are doing celibacy now. Guys, too. It clears the mind and channels the energy. I'll stick with it unless somebody comes along that I really relate to, or maybe even then. It might be interesting to live with someone without having total sex."

Frances wondered how much sex was total, but didn't like to ask. Hallie explained, "I mean genital sex."

It hadn't occurred to Frances that the body could be divided into sexual and non-sexual areas. Then what was the touch of Erika's hand on her hair or a passing pat? She said judiciously, "I suppose that was due to happen — the pendulum swings back. All right, you do eat eggs, don't you? We'll expect you around six."

Hallie smiled. She was tall and slender, olive-skinned, her dark hair held in place by a beaded band. Frances asked, "Are you an Indian?"

"Me? My father was Croatian and my mother was an old-line Yankee from Vermont. I grew up on one of those little farms where they sharpen the sheep's noses so they can graze between the stones." She considered. "I suppose I could have some Indian blood. A lot of those old-timers married into the Oneida and Naragansett. You know the Oneida are trying to get millions of dollars from the government for the land they lost when the Kinzua dam was built. Some government — George Washington signed that treaty, but it didn't do the Indians any good. They lost their tribal lands anyhow."

"I hope they get something out of it." Frances wondered how a half-Croatian, half-Yankee had gotten from Vermont to Arizona, but she knew better than to ask. The answer would have been, "hitchhiking and Greyhound." That wasn't the journey she had in mind. What thoughts, what desires had landed Hallie here and not in Algeria or Alaska or some other place? Perhaps she hadn't analyzed it herself. The world was full of drifting youngsters looking for something, not sure what it was they wanted but confident that they would recognize it when they found it. They existed precariously on the edge of a social order they rejected, in a kind of casual shifting fellowship.

I wish I were thirty years younger, she thought. I don't know that I want to live that way, but I'd like a chance to choose. She put down the bit of fabric she was holding and smiled at Hallie. "We'll see you Sunday." And walked out of the shop musing, as so often these days, in the changes she had seen and the way human experience kept repeating itself, with different details, but the same underlying pattern. In the twenties it was Paris — it was Taos and Carmel. Now, it was wandering all over the world with some kind of skill that would get them by from day to day.

She wondered where Kim was and what she was doing. What would happen to Carol and her friends, who were beginning to scatter; Peg and Mountaintop were gone, the adobe house was beginning to crumble. She would stay in Arizona, probably, for the rest of her life. That was all right. It was what she wanted. But she thought about the young ones with vague envy, even while she felt a sort of parental concern for them. We came along at a strange time in history, Erika and I. Too late for the firebrand women, Susan B. Anthony and the Blackwells, for Emma Goldman and all the socialists, anarchists, single taxers, and suffragettes, the women who were going to turn the world upside-down. Too early to strike out for freedom the way the young ones are doing now. Maybe we're middle-class, maybe we brought too many of the old values with us — but they're nice to live with.

Maybe we're supposed to be a bridge between the generations.

Or maybe all this doesn't make any sense. We just go along from day to day, and things change around us while we're looking the other way. Maybe there really isn't any pattern.

By this time she had reached home. She picked the mail out of the RFD box, noticed that Mr. Marcussen was out playing with the dog, and went in to see what Erika was doing and what they were having for supper. Erika was the Saturday cook by virtue of having the day off.

We really are in a rut, Frances thought.

TWENTY-THREE

It was one of those luminous days so rare in the southwest: a sky clear blue without glare, unlimited visibility, and a light breeze. Erika stopped to look out of the schoolhouse door before she went into the staff lounge for a cup of instant coffee. She knew what she would see; three of the teachers sitting in front of the portable TV, avidly listening to whichever newscaster was rehashing the details of the Watergate investigation. Pictures of Ehrlichman and Haldeman filled the upper right-hand corner of the lighted screen. "Rosencrantz and Gildenstern," the second-grade teacher said, making a place for her on the sofa. "I don't know why I'm watching this stuff. I saw it all this morning."

"How do you feel about it?"

"Sick at my stomach, but not surprised. I campaigned for McGovern, you may or may not remember."

"I voted for him."

Melanie Lane said, "I voted for Nixon. I wouldn't have if I'd known it was going to turn out like this."

And what made you think he'd turn out any other way? Erika wondered silently. Most of the time she tried to maintain a neutral position on any issue that didn't directly affect the school system, but she had worn a McGovern button all through the 1972 campaign, although she didn't discuss the election except on home ground and on her own time. She mixed a cup of coffee, drank it quickly, and excused herself.

If this weather held, she and Frances might drive out into the desert tomorrow; it would be Saturday and Frances had the day off too. Or they might pack a picnic lunch and take it to the park. Never mind that they ought to go to the laundromat, the kitchen floor needed mopping, and the freezer was almost empty. It was smart to enjoy the good weather while it held, before summer's intense heat set in; and it would be good to get away from the television and newspapers for a while.

In all the excitement over the investigation, it was hard to focus on anything else. She knew that her teachers were doing their best to get through the day's scheduled work, but even the little children in kindergarten were boiling over with the morning's revelations in two languages. It kept popping up in arithmetic and reading classes as well as in social studies, where it more or less belonged. At least, Erika thought, the kids were learning an important lesson: not to trust politicians. Maybe a little cynicism, developed early enough, would keep them from voting for the kind of people their parents had rushed to elect.

The desk phone rang. She picked it up. Barbara's voice said, "Erika, are you free for lunch? I've got something to talk over with you."

"Make it a quickie. I can spare forty-five minutes."

"Okay. Can you stand the corner place? I'll order for you, I'm there already."

Erika said, "BLT and a cup of Sanka." She was used to Barbara's enthusiasms and anxieties; they seldom amounted to much. She locked her desk and walked out into the mellow light. Either Barbara and Kathy had had a fight, or one of them had a protégée, or she was collecting money for a good cause. If we gave to all her projects, we'd starve, Erika thought, steeling herself to say *no*. She took a deep, appreciative breath before she went into the smoky little cafe.

Whatever Barbara had on her mind, it wasn't anything that involved human need. Her face was calm and she bit into her sandwich as though she hadn't eaten for a while. The early lunch and late coffee break customers had left; they were almost alone in the room except for the waitress, who was doubling as cashier. Barbara took a long swallow of iced tea. "I met with a group in Phoenix last night. They're planning a parade for Gay Pride Week. I'd like to see a good-sized group from Tucson there. I suppose you and Frances wouldn't consider going?"

"You suppose right."

"I know you don't belong to any gay groups, any organizations that will be there. I know you're cautious. But there comes a time—"

"There will be newspaper coverage. Maybe TV. It's different for the bar people, they don't have that much to lose. And the ones who are in business for themselves." She was rationalizing, and she knew it. The thought of coming out at a public rally was panic-making. State Representative Robert W. Ollenfield and his social wife were sure to be among those watching the newscasts and reading the papers. Since Bob's election to the state legislature in '72, Frances had been nervous about the possibility of a confrontation. I am not going to expose her, Erika thought.

"We really need people to be on the planning committee —work out the details, sort of. You could do that."

"You're not asking us to march?"

"Sure I am, but if you won't, you won't. I respect your reasons." Like hell you do, Erika said silently. "I don't want you to put your job on the line, but we sure could use you on the executive committee."

"This is a fine surprise to spring on a person. I haven't even thought about Gay Pride Week. I know they march in New York and San Francisco—"

"And Podunk, Gopher Prairie. I can see you don't like the idea."

"It's fine for the young," Erika said firmly. "It would be nice to see more women in it—so far it's been mostly men. I suppose the lunatic fringe will boycott it." She bit into her sandwich, though she wasn't hungry. "I'd like to see a time when people would do whatever they want—when gays could parade like Cinco de Mayo or St. Patrick's Day. I just don't like the idea of gay people getting out and yelling 'Look at us!' especially if half of them are in high drag, getting laughed at and hissed. Last year in Chicago, hoodlums went up on the roofs and threw eggs at them."

"Is that a reason or an excuse?"

"Both," Erika admitted. "I don't want to come out to everybody or under all circumstances. I also don't think the people who turn out will represent, well, people like Fran and me. Maybe they would in a place like San Francisco, maybe there would be professionals, white-collar people, but not here."

"You don't want to risk your job, of course."

"It's not just money. I've put the best years of my life into this system. It means something to me. I think I'm doing as much as I can within the limitations of the system. The bilingual program is under way. We're working on classes for handicapped kids — that's going to mean politicking, maybe a bond issue. If we're lucky we may get better nutrition on the lunch program. I don't have any right to jeopardize all that for my own satisfaction."

Barbara's glow had dimmed. "You won't help at all?"

"I'll work on the planning committee if you promise not to use my name in the mailings. Behind the scenes. I can't speak for Fran, she makes her own decisions. You'll have to talk to her."

"Well, thanks."

"I have to go."

She left, stopping at the cash register to pay for her uneaten sandwich. Barbara sat looking after her.

Walking briskly back to the school, Erika tried to justify her decision to herself. She loved Barbara, her energy and dedication, but she wasn't going to feel guilty. It's not as though the whole future of the gay liberation movement depended on my getting out there and marching, she thought crossly. The young ones really do lay it on you. They can't be penalized — no, that's not true, Debby and Catherine, everyone knows they're a pair. I know about them and I'm sure they know about me, but they'll never say anything. Her face softened at the thought of her two young teachers who shared an apartment and went quietly about their own business. There were thousands like them, trying to find a workable compromise between security and happiness.

"It ought not be that way," she told Frances after dinner that evening. They had eaten on the patio, enjoying their latest buy — a table and chairs in glass and white enamel leaves. The sun was going down in a flush of pink and apricot; birds chirped in the mulberry tree.

"People ought to be able to live their personal lives any way they want to."

"Ought to isn't is."

"Barb is so dedicated."

"So are you."

"Well, I believe in gay liberation."

"That's all right. She believes in teaching."

"It's not her top-priority thing."

"It isn't mine, either. I'm more interested in getting Julian Lopez back on his feet, walking without crutches. What would it take to make you come out?" Frances propped her elbows on the table and looked intently at Erika. "What would be urgent enough?"

"I suppose if we were threatened massively — something like the fugitive slave law, not just picky little local ordinances. Or if they started burning us for witches, like in the old days. You know, a lot of the women who were executed in the middle ages were accused of being lesbians. They were the uppity ones." Frances smiled. "I just don't want to give up everything I've accomplished, to make myself feel good."

"Ignorance and stupidity are cumulative," Frances said thoughtfully. "The world is run by stupid, ignorant, greedy people. Look at the bastards who are being pushed out into the light of day in Washington — they're the same ones that persecuted — "

"Prosecuted."

"I mean persecuted — some of the greatest artists in this country, a few years ago. Nixon was on their damned committee — he volunteered for it. They all took corruption for granted. Why should you be surprised now?"

Erika's mind was not on Watergate nor on the McCarthy days. "I told her I'd work on her committee if there wasn't any publicity involved."

"We could give some money for printing, and so on."

"It's not the same thing."

"I'd march if all the gays in the hospital would. God knows there are enough of them."

They sat silent while the sunlight faded and the evening breeze sprang up. At least she hasn't thought about Bob, Erika thought. Or has she? It took a while to find out what was bothering Frances; her worries simmered for a while, gathering steam until they exploded.

She put a tentative arm around Frances. "I'm glad for the kids. They have groups to belong to, they have magazines and books. Remember when all we had was the good old *Ladder*, in a plain brown wrapper? Remember how we passed around *The Well of Loneliness*? Now they know when they meet somebody—all right, she's gay, they don't have to poke and prod and be scared to death. But we have something the young ones don't."

"Wrinkles," Frances suggested. "Saggy boobs and gray hair."

"That's surface stuff. We know where we've come from."

"Well, yes. But wouldn't you like to be twenty again? Didn't you ever fantasize some liberated young girl in your bed?"

"I've tried, but she always turns into you." She unbuttoned the front of Frances' shirt and dropped it to the floor. The patio was in deep shadow now. "I like these even if they do sag a little."

"Oh, in that case I have other things that are even more interesting."

"Old age requires an innerspring mattress," Erika said firmly. "And no neighbors shining their headlights on us, if they should come home. Let's adjourn indoors."

In the dusky kitchen Frances dropped her slacks to the floor and stepped out of her cotton underpants. Lately she had been undressing with some reluctance—her belly sagged a little, her thighs were no longer smooth. But the love and tenderness in Erika's touch were unmistakable.

"Come to bed," Erika said. She ran her hands over Frances' breasts, down her belly, found what she was seeking and inserted a questing finger. "Your hair doesn't match," she said. It was too dark to see her smile but Frances could hear it in her voice. "You have an old head and a young cunt—come to bed, my matchless love. That's a joke."

"No, it isn't. You mean every word of it."

"That's right. You are one of a kind."

They walked into the bedroom laced together, as if drawing all their strength from touch. "Isn't it nice that there's no limit on love?" Erika pulled her down on top of the bedspread. "Love's not time's fool. Shakespeare said so."

"It must be so, then." She pulled the whole length of Erika against her. "Love me then, darling. Don't ever stop."

TWENTY-FOUR

"Seems to me election year comes around oftener than it used to."

"Everything comes around oftener, except payday. Why?"

"It's so different this time; I mean, four years ago we had someone to vote for. McGovern was going to end the war. This time I really don't give a damn."

"Well, look," Erika said, "on one hand, you have a peanut farmer who's been a southern governor and has too many teeth, and on the other you have a dumb jock. I'm tired of voting against, I'd like to vote *for* something."

"At least the gay issue is out in the open."

"Sure. The Dems will sound tolerant as all hell in their press conferences, but they won't put a gay plank in their platform. The Reps won't commit themselves. Candidates who want the liberal vote will make it clear that they personally are straight."

Frances said, sounding tired, "I wish we'd moved to Canada." For they had inquired into immigration stipulations when so many young men were trying to escape the undeclared war. The reversion into barbarism, Frances thought, was slower there than in the States.

"We're too old now to be desirable emigrants. Also, it gets cold in the winter. I wouldn't mind living in Quebec, never mind the political rumpus, but I'd never learn to speak their kind of French. I suppose we could try Mexico."

"No hiding place down there, either. I'll end up voting for the peanut farmer, unless the Socialists come up with someone terrific."

"Gene Debs has been dead for a long time."

Erika propped the last plate in the drying rack and rinsed out her plastic sponge. The kitchen glittered with order and fresh paint. It was usually livable, that was about all that could be said for it, but this spit and polish in the wake of decorating was impressive and she was going to appreciate it while it lasted. Frances shook two E capsules into her water-pinked hand. "I read somewhere about why time telescopes as you get older. The brain works like a memory bank — the more data you store in it, the less important each separate item gets. Like when you're a kid, from Christmas to Christmas seems like forever. When you get old, every day gets smaller. Sunday supplement science," she admitted, smiling at her own gullibility.

"The man that figured that out may have a mind like a memory bank. Mine's more like a sieve, or whasisname's hall closet in the old days."

Erika switched off the overhead light. They trailed into the living room, which was scheduled for a makeover as soon as they could get around to it, but was still comfortably untidy. Frances stooped down into the wing chair and kicked off her zori. "What's on the tube, more politics? Anyway let's see if they cover the local ERA rally."

"This is Monday. You want a blow-by-blow account of the city council meeting?" Erika turned the dial. A pleasant-looking young man materialized on the screen. Frances said, "Let's just listen to the headlines and go to bed."

"Is this a declaration of passion?"

"Fatigue."

The newscaster smiled. "With all the focus on the national scene, it's easy to overlook local and state events. Arizona will have one interesting campaign this fall. Robert W. Ollenfield has announced his intention of trying for the seat in the state legislature now held by Francis Chance. Ollenfield, head of the Phoenix branch of Plastix Produx, a firm employing about five hundred people, was appointed last year to finish out the term of the late Dorothy Gibson. This will be his first campaign for an elected office. Formerly from New Mexico and originally from Illinois, where his father founded Plastix Produx, Ollenfield and his family have resided in Phoenix for about three years. He is active in the Rotary Club, Masons, and Better Business Bureau, and has served in the Phoenix Chamber of Commerce for several months. Chance left the seat vacant when he announced his forthcoming retirement due to ill health. (Erika grinned. Chance had been caught with his hand in the cash register once too often, and the Tucson papers, in their inter-city rivalry, had made the most of it.) Interviewed by reporters, Ollenfield said, 'Well, I'm sure of two votes, mine and my wife's. My daughter's ready to hit the campaign trail, but she's only sixteen.' "

Frances said, awed, "My God."

"He'll never get it."

"He just might, if they can split the vote. He hasn't been around long enough to make enemies." For the moment she had forgotten who Bob was: this was a political issue.

Erika's face reminded her. Erika said, "Look, he's not a kid any more, he's a businessman with clout, he's been around long enough to know what he wants, and from the evidence he's got a pretty good notion of how to get it." She switched off the set. "I have a feeling that the city council meeting could be an anticlimax. Let's go to bed."

It wasn't that simple. Bob's face was on the front page of the morning paper, a rather heavy, bland face that might have belonged to any of the younger crop of politicians. Erika said, "He certainly doesn't look like you. Does he look like his father?"

"How would I know? I haven't seen either of them for six-teen years."

"At least you're not in any danger of being connected with the campaign — nobody knows you're related. You're a Kirby, legally — and that's a common enough name." Erika frowned. "No nostalgia, now. What's past is past. It hasn't anything to do with you."

"It isn't going to be easy."

It wasn't. I'll stop reading the papers till after the election, Frances determined as she drove to work. I don't know that man, that businessman getting on for middle age, with thin-ning hair and a thickening waistline — I don't know his social wife or his teenage daughter. All right, he was a cute little boy. Hitler was somebody's cute little boy.

The trouble was, she kept remembering Bob's wedding day. People. Music. Bill half loaded but calm and stern. Bob pale, Mari calm in her long satin dress and billowy veil. Herself in the front row, her black eye not quite disguised by pancake makeup and her stomach churning. A bar brawl followed by a night in jail wasn't the best preparation for a family wedding, she told herself now, seventeen years later — almost seventeen years, anyway.

I went to that church under the impression that I was saying goodbye to Bake and the gay scene because of Bob, she thought. What I was really doing was saying goodbye to him — and my marriage, the house on Commonwealth Avenue and all the rest of it. I hadn't even met Erika, then.

Even if Bob had been sympathetic towards her, even if he had been able to understand her viewpoint (which no one had explained to him), there was Mari, sweet and cool as a plate of lemon sherbet. Mari would be the one who made the decisions in that family; she had understood that by the time the minister got through saying "Dearly Beloved." No, that wedding day was the one that split her life into two distinct parts — Before Erika and After Erika, though she hadn't known it at the time.

And the girl is sixteen. My granddaughter. Isabel, a pretty name. I wonder what she's like. I'd probably have been one hell of a bad grandmother — I'll never know.

Leave your personal affairs at the door when you go to work.

She got through the day somehow, and went to the movies with Erika after supper — an indulgence they seldom allowed themselves partly because there wasn't time in their lives and partly because good films were fairly scarce. They were in bed by ten-thirty.

It was the next day that the Kromek thing broke.

Something was wrong. That was plain as soon as she got inside the hospital door. It was in the air, in the way the receptionist looked at her. The panic that lies just below the surface of any closeted lesbian life leaped into being: someone has found out about me and Erika, someone has made a charge. Then: it's about Bob. She said "Good morning," mechanically, went on her way, and was stopped by one of the young nurses. "The Kromek kid's waiting for you in the PT office. She came in looking like the wrath of God, bawling, and said she had to see you." She looked inquiringly at Frances: what was going on between Kirby and the Kromek kid? Frances said, "I'm not sure — she's one of the aides, isn't she? Tall kid with long hair?"

"That's the one."

Frances laughed. "Probably something world-shaking, like she broke a thermometer."

The aides ranged from sixteen to nineteen years of age, some of them still in high school, some filling in time until they could find jobs. Full of romantic ideas about nursing, they were likely to get jittery over small mistakes. Frances hoped it wasn't in the patient's mouth, or any other orifice at the time. But why come to her and not the charge nurse or the supervisor?

If you were in the fifties, the kids assumed you knew everything. Flip as they acted, there were times when they were grateful for authority. Surrogate parent, they wanted — I never volunteered for it, and anyhow you're the same person at sixty that you were at twenty, only with trifocals and arthritis.

The Kromek kid was looking out the window, and when she turned, Frances saw that she did look like the wrath of God — at least, if you believed in that kind of God. Her pink-striped pinafore was clean and crisp, but she had a black eye and a darkening bruise on her left cheek. She jumped as the door opened and then seeing who it was, looked relieved. "Miss Kirby, I've got to talk to you, I've got to talk to somebody. I don't know what to do, I feel like I'm going crazy and I can't go home. I don't know what to do."

"Slow down." Frances dropped into the desk chair, the seat of authority. "Sit down. Take a deep breath. Now — start at the beginning and tell me what's happened to you."

"I went out with this fellow, Chuck. I've known him a long time, our folks go to the same church and I thought it would be all right to go out with him. I don't like boys, but my mom keeps yelling at me, go out with some nice fellow. Go to the movies, you want to be an old maid? Sure I do, but she'd have a fit if I said so. So, all right, I went to the movies." Frances was beginning to despair of getting a coherent story out of her. She took a deep breath, and a firm grip on her patience. She had a pretty good idea of what had happened. Who the hell does she think I am — Dear Abby?

"We went to the drive-in, and it was all right, only he pawed around at me, and then he took me home, only he parked a couple doors down the street, and when I went to get out he pulled me back in. I thought he wanted to kiss me. Guys do expect to kiss you if they spend movie money on you." She shivered. "I tried not to mind it. Then he put his hand down my front, you know how they do." Frances remembered how they did, and closed her eyes in anticipation of what was coming, but the image on her inner lids was sharp and detailed. "I told him to quit, and then I tried to get out of the car, but he tripped me up with his foot and then he grabbed me and he knocked me back against the back of the seat and unbuttoned my shorts — "

She stopped, and looked at Frances for help.

"And unzipped his shorts and raped you."

"How did you know?"

To you? Kromek's eyes asked. The answer leaped up in Frances: only by my husband. She looked at the top of her desk. "And I went in. My dad was in the kitchen, he hadn't gone to bed yet, and he started to yell at me. The zipper on my shorts was broke. So he started to yell at me. Mom came downstairs in her nightgown and she started yelling too, she said I was a tramp and a no-good and I could pack up my clothes and get out of there till I was willing to behave myself. I only went with him because she made me."

"Did you tell them what happened?"

"My dad said I must have asked for it. A nice Catholic boy like Chuck wouldn't do something like that unless I tempted him."

"Did anybody call the police?"

"I was scared. I took a bath and got ready to go out — it was around three, I noticed the clock in the kitchen. My dad

grabbed me when I started to leave. He slapped me around—
he's always been strong on hitting us, but not like that. When
he let me go I went back upstairs and put on my uniform and
I came down to the hospital and sat on the steps till the seven
o'clock shift came in."

"Have you seen a doctor?"

The girl shook her head.

"Suppose you're pregnant?"

"I'll kill myself." Hilda's face reddened. "I'd rather die. I
don't like fellows anyhow, that was what made my mother mad,
she kept saying I was queer. I am, I guess. I never knew about
it till a year ago, then I found a book in the library and I thought,
uh huh, that's me, that's the way I am. I'm always in love with
some girl, only I never knew what to do about it. So when my
mom—I don't want her to know. That's why I went with him.
Only I didn't expect anything like what happened."

Some mother, Frances thought. Hilda picked up on it. "She
never told me nothing. When I got my period I was so scared,
I thought I was bleeding to death, maybe I had cancer or something, you know? She gets mad if you ask her anything. She
keeps saying I'll know it all when I get married. But I don't
want to marry anybody. She don't listen."

In this day and age, Frances thought, and they try to tell
us we don't need sex education in the schools—no it's the
parents' responsibility. The kids act so cool, you think they
know everything, and here they are all churned up. So vulnerable, no smarter really than we were at that age. Seeing mice
born in the first grade is no answer.

"You better go down to GYN and tell them exactly what
happened. They'll do a D and C and give you an antibiotic
shot. I'll go with you."

"I feel so ashamed."

"You feel ashamed? That Chuck's the one to feel ashamed."
She took Hilda's resisting arm and propelled her to the door.
Hilda stopped on the threshold. "That book said there are other
people like me in New York, but I don't have any way to get
there."

"There are a lot of people like you everywhere."

"They say, the kids say, that you, that — that's why I wanted to ask you."

Denial trembled on the tip of Frances' tongue. It was so easy to lie, or to look blank and not understand. Oh, really, who says so? Some people know a lot that's not so. Choosing among phrases, she heard herself say, "I am. It's not always easy."

"But possible?"

"Sure, it's possible."

"You have someone."

"Yes." She thought of Erika, in all this clutter of feelings and happenings. "Come on, now. Dr. Sanchez is a nice man, a kind man. He won't hurt you and he'll make you safe." Thinking, those damned stirrups, and the panic.

Hilda said again, shrinking almost visibly. "I'm so ashamed."

"What for? You haven't done anything — would you be ashamed if someone broke your arm? Sanchez will have to report it, you might have to talk to the police — if you do, just tell them the whole thing exactly the way it happened. Let them charge the guy if they want to. It might make him think twice the next time — it might save some other girl from being roughed up." And the millennium might come tomorrow, she jeered at herself, but it won't hurt to hope.

"He said don't tell anybody."

"Big deal. Come on, let's get it over with. I'm supposed to be working."

She left Hilda at Dr. Sanchez's door. "You better come home with me for a few days. We've got a spare bedroom."

She explained the situation to Sanchez, who looked sorrowful but not surprised, and left Hilda alone with him in a state of unreasoning terror.

All of a sudden I'm a surrogate mother, she thought wryly, getting her first old lady onto the massage table. Well, what am I supposed to do, let the kid sleep on a park bench? We'll have the police knocking at the door, the parents, maybe newspaper reporters — not that rape is a novelty these days, they got a seventy-three-year-old woman a couple weeks ago. Can't be helped. I wouldn't mind giving the mother a piece of my mind.

There was no time to think about Bob Ollenfield and his political ambitions. She was aware of a buzz of gossip, explained briefly what had happened, was glad to note that the women on the staff were furious at Chuck and ready to sympathize with Hilda. The hospital got its share of such cases, and the kid was one of their own. Mostly, she wondered what Erika would say when she turned up with a houseguest, whether they had clean sheets for an extra bed, whether Sanchez would give her a prescription for sedatives if they were needed, and what she would say when the kid felt well enough for a lecture course in lesbianism. She didn't doubt that one would be called for.

Erika, as might have been expected, took the whole thing calmly. Frances knew she was seething with fury at the un-known Chuck—by this time he had so many enemies that the heat of their anger should have burned him to the soul, suppos-ing he had one—but Erika smiled at Hilda and said, "It'll be nice to have you here for a while. I hope you like soup, because it's what we're having." You could count on Erika. She would have risen cool and calm at the Last Trump, and invited Gab-riel to dinner.

Hilda's eyes widened. "Gee, Miss Frohmann, I heard you make a speech once, when my kid sister graduated eighth grade."

Oh, God, now she not only knows about me, she knows about my partner in whatever you want to call it. Not that any-body would be surprised, but guessing at something and know-ing it are different things. These kids are blabbermouths. Can't be helped. She said, "You two get acquainted. I'll set the table."

They were looking each other over. Poor Erika, all this on top of a day's work.

Hilda wasn't hungry. The reaction from pain, panic, and loss of sleep had set in and her eyelids were heavy before she finished the meal. Frances gave her a Seconal anyway and found her a pair of pajamas. "We'll be right in the next room if you wake up in the night. Otherwise we'll see you in the morning. You won't mind making your own breakfast, will you?" She brought Hilda a glass of water, tucked in the covers, and gave her a light kiss on the cheek. "Don't be worried if you wake sort of depressed. It's the medicine."

Erika was washing the soup bowls. "Now tell me what happened, if you don't mind. The girl looks like she was hit by a truck."

"I tried to call," Frances apologized, "but you were in that damned meeting. She collided with a guy who took her to the movies, raped her, and left her in her folks' driveway. Folks went through the old never-darken-my-door routine. I didn't know what else to do with her."

"You did right. So why are you looking so guilty?"

"She's gay. At least, she thinks she is. She was trying to keep it from her parents—from herself too, I guess. She spilled it to me because she had picked up a notion that I'm one of those. I couldn't think up a good lie on the spur of the moment. I only hope she won't describe all the details of our domestic life when she gets back to work."

"She may not want to go back. If she's homeless she may have to look for a paid job—candy-stripers are volunteers, aren't they? Anyhow it was bound to happen sooner or later. I suppose she's been scraped?"

"Sanchez fixed her up. He may have called the cops—I didn't ask. I'd just as soon she didn't press any charges," Frances admitted. "To be PC I ought to hope they'll get the guy and throw him in the slammer. How do you keep him from going after somebody else, otherwise? For myself, I wish the whole thing would just go away."

"It's her decision."

"We're probably worrying about nothing. These things happen—most of the time they don't even get in the paper." Frances lapsed into brooding. "It's all ambiguous," she added after a moment's silence. "Used to be a mere suspicion of homosexuality was enough to ruin you, theoretically, yet lots of people had relationships and it was all right as long as they didn't come out in the open. If anybody verbalized it—remember those pathetic teachers in The Children's Hour? Now it's on TV and in magazines, and you never know where you are. It's like being black in the north."

The police did telephone the next evening, having called the hospital and found out where Hilda was staying. She was panicked. "I don't want to talk to them. Do I have to?"

"No, but if you don't, he may try it on some other girl."

"I think he knew there was something wrong with me."

"There's nothing wrong with you," Frances said, not too patiently. "You're a lesbian, like one-tenth of all the women in the world. And some of the other nine-tenths have tried it. You might as well say there's something wrong with being left-handed. They used to kill left-handed kids, thought it was a sign of devil possession."

Erika said briefly, "Remember, you're the victim. Chuck is the one who did wrong."

The police showed up after supper. One was young and male; the other, young and female and, Frances was pretty sure, gay. They accepted coffee and settled down to a routine questioning. The man asked a few factual questions and his partner jotted down the answers. "Now if you'll sign this."

"I don't want to go to court."

The officer sighed. "That's what they all say. How are we going to get these turkeys off the street if nobody presses charges? We get called in on husband and wife fights, she calls up and asks for protection, then she won't sign the papers and she never shows up in court, and six months later she turns up with another black eye and a broken jaw."

Hilda said stubbornly, "I don't want to see him."

"Do you think you're the only one it ever happened to? It's an accident, like breaking a leg. It'll be all right."

The young man said, "Yeah, you'll fall in love with some nice guy and he won't mind." The four women looked at him.

After the officers left, Frances said with fake cheerfulness, "Sanchez says why don't you come back to work. You're his favorite candy-striper, he says."

"I wish I didn't ever have to go back. Everybody knows."

"What would you like to do?"

"Go someplace far away from here and get a job. I don't want to see my folks, either."

Frances and Erika exchanged glances. With all good will, they had missed their privacy. If the kid stayed in Tucson she would be leaning on them for advice and companionship; perhaps for money help as well. They wished her well, but they weren't ready to adopt her. There was probably enough talk already.

Erika asked slowly, "Would you like to go to San Francisco? We have friends there you could stay with for a while —they know a lot of women, they could help you find work. San Francisco is a good place for finding jobs." A good place for finding lovers too, she added silently. There's some risk in that, but with a good support group to pick up the pieces—

"Sure, that sounds all right."

"I wouldn't be eighteen again for anything in the world," Frances said when they were getting ready for bed.

"Don't worry, you won't have a chance to be. I must say it's tiring having an extra person in the house. I can feel her listening through the wall."

"Is that why we've been sleeping on opposite sides of the bed?"

"You'll see."

TWENTY-FIVE

1980 was a newsworthy year.

The nation went through the promises and recriminations of another presidential election and, bored with the platitudes of the peanut farmer, elected an aging second-rate actor to its highest office. His first act was to cut all the appropriations for human welfare: food stamps, day care, school lunch programs, low-cost medical care, housing programs, and scientific research. His second was to buy a two-hundred-thousand-dollar set of dishes and order cowboy boots bearing the Presidential Seal, at a thousand dollars a pair. Old people were assured there would be no cuts in Social Security, which set some of them to wondering. "It's not only inhuman, it's vulgar," Erika said angrily. "Now he's going to increase the military budget without raising taxes. Orwell overlooked that one."

A radio evangelist admitted making more than fifty million dollars a year, some of it from old people trying to cope with the rising cost of living. "I suppose they want some kind of security, and they're sure not going to find it in this life." Barbara mused. Another organized something called the Moral Majority, dedicated to doing away with legal abortion and removing from the shelves of libraries all books that depicted people acting like human beings. For some reason, the biblical accounts of rape, murder, incest, and pillage were exempted from this censorship. Arizona's senior senator had a few pungent comments to make on that, and made them.

Things were popping on the local scene, too. A popular football coach was accused of mishandling university funds and was hotly defended by alumni who thought that he was probably guilty but liked him because his teams won more games than they lost. Two ranchers, brothers, were arrested for beating and chaining their illegal Mexican hired hands. They were defended in court by different lawyers, the result being that one was convicted and the other acquitted. "Darrow was right," Erika said, "Justice is how good a lawyer can you afford?"

Erika was eyebrow-deep in the Navaho–Hopi land dispute, which seemed to be carried on chiefly between rival factions of whites with large real estate interests. As far as Frances could see, the Navajo were the only Indians in the southwest who hadn't been done out of their property. "The rest are all hungry and helpless, whereas they've built up the tribal income, they went commercial early on. They make blankets and jewelry, they educate the smart kids and those kids put part of their income back into the tribe—so now the sharpies are determined to take away their grazing land. And their holy places, the centers of their religion." She also said that she was less concerned about her own soul, or anybody else's, than about the eighteen interballistic missiles ranged around the city. "Let one of those blow, and your soul will go right up along with the rest of you."

Bob Ollenfield had served in the state legislature six years without either disgracing or distinguishing himself, and was running again. Now and then, when nothing more exciting was available, he made the Tucson papers. State Representative Addresses Rotary. Mr. and Mrs. Ollenfield Attend Opera. Mari was still slender, chic, and glacial. Frances supposed she herself might have been spared all this if she had stayed in Illinois; his fame was local and limited. (She could see Mari's calculating eye turned on the White House, but guessed that Bob lacked the ambition.) He seemed to have all the ingredients for success: good looks, enough money, enough intelligence but not too much, and a gift for not making waves. A good, second-rate politician. "We'll be seeing him in *People* one of these days."

Erika asked ironically, "Do you begrudge him his little hour in the sun?"

"Not if it's what he wants. It can't be worse than being dedicated to Plastix Produx."

"At least he's not a lush."

"She wouldn't let him be."

"You had him till he was nineteen. Look at all the mothers who never get to see their kids grow up."

"That's no help."

They were on her mind these days, those lesbian mothers whose children were wrenched away from them by male judges, all those women who had to choose between their children and their lovers, knowing they were going to lose either way. Victimized by vindictive or honestly bewildered men who saw them as perverted or irrational, they plodded through life. Lili, whose three little girls lived in Florida with their father, was a newcomer to the Sunday supper group.

"They'll be all right. He's a good father, as good as he knows how to be. I could stand it if he would only let me have them for vacations."

"Did you ever consider just keeping your mouth shut and not making an issue of it?"

"Seeing Bet behind his back? It wouldn't have worked. I felt sick every time I had to go to bed with him. Anyway, he found her letters, snooping through my dresser."

Bet asked defensively, "How could she be a good mother when she wasn't fulfilled as a person?"

"That's what liberation is about. You can't be a good wife or mother or employee or anything until you find out who you are. That's hard enough for the heteros, but at least they're making some headway. If you're gay you're several squares behind the starting line."

"We're making headway."

"Yeah, a centimeter at a time."

Magazines came and went in the feminist bookstore: *Sinister Wisdom*, *Big Mama Rag*, *Amazon*, *Off Our Backs*, *Countrywoman*, all descended from *The Ladder*. *The Ladder* was history — herstory — now. Three volumes of gleanings from it stood on Erika's bookshelves alongside Isabel Miller, Rita Mae Brown, Jane Rule, Kate Millett, June Arnold. Now and then a magazine article touched on the subject. A nationwide television program starred a lesbian mother who had won custody of two small daughters. She and her lover were thoroughly middle-class, had a story to tell, and knew the public needed to be educated.

Bet said again, "We're getting there. Some of us. They don't tell you about the losers, the ones that lose their children—or their parents. My mother won't speak to me. I called her last Christmas: when she heard my voice she hung up. Not that I care, it's her loss. Lili's going to sue for custody as soon as we have some money. We haven't given up. I love those kids almost as much as she does."

Lili said, trying to smile, "The girls are old enough to remember me. They know I care about them, even if we lose. That's something."

Erika mused, "Isn't it strange? Anything goes. Wife-swapping—why don't they ever call it husband-swapping, do you suppose? Open marriage and group sex. It's simply taken for granted that young people will live together for a while before they marry. Maybe the next step will be to do away with marriage altogether, and won't that be a blow to the advertising industry! The straights are changing in so many ways I can't keep up, and we're about fifty years behind the times."

"At least we're rid of the old femme-butch nonsense."

Variation on a theme, Frances thought, every gathering these days came back to gay rights and the feminist struggle—when will we learn to fight alongside our hetero sisters? At breakfast on a sunny Sunday morning, she said, "It's silly to be so touchy about Bob. He's over forty, he's built the life he wants. I'm acting like those dear little old gray-haired mothers in the ads. Send her a Hallmark card and she's off your back for another year."

"Weeping with joy because the kids called long distance and Ma Bell made another dollar."

"There are times when I suspect you of being cynical."

Erika said soberly, "I still dream about my mother once in a while. She was so gentle."

"People ought to be nicer to each other. Not just families, or maybe everybody's a family. Sounds so pious. Anyhow, I didn't give up Bob for you. I didn't know you were alive. I didn't think I could go on. Of course I'd have liked to know you then, it was in the back of my mind that there might be somebody, but I didn't know it was going to be you."

Erika reached for the coffeepot, which stood on a trivet in the middle of the table, and refilled both cups. "You sound a little confused. Let's go to the swap meet. I need a screwdriver and a pair of ski boots."

"What in heaven's name for?"

"My seventh grade is putting on a play."

It was a good enough excuse for going to the swap meet, which they both relished for its diversity and unexpectedness. Erika said it was like a medieval marketplace and she wouldn't be surprised if a troupe of wandering minstrels strolled in with lute and sackbuts, whatever those were. In fact there was usually a bearded boy playing guitar with a hopeful cap at his feet, and instead of an ox roasting on its spit, you could buy a barbecue from the tailgate of a truck.

Frances pushed back her chair. "Let's leave the dishes. Barb got a whole stack of Christies last week for fifty cents."

"You've read all of Christie."

"I keep forgetting how they come out. We saw *Murder on the Nile* on TV, remember, and I never did figure out who killed him."

New tissue grows over scars, Erika thought. Pick at them, and they hurt. Ignore them and they might fade out. Still, she suggested, "You could write to Bob at his office if you really wanted to. I suppose Mari reads his home mail."

"Reads it all. She's working in his office until the campaign's over."

"Forget it, then."

It would have been easier to forget if the *Star* hadn't carried a picture of Isabel, just before Frances' sixty-third birthday. "Isabel Ollenfield, daughter of state representative Robert W. Ollenfield, has registered at the U of A for her senior year. At his press conference yesterday her father said, 'It's a fine school and I am pleased that she has chosen to earn her degree there.' "

"More votes from Pima County." Erika said. "She looks like you."

"She's better-looking than I ever was."

"No, she looks like you. Cut her out and paste her in your memory book if you want to, only don't brood."

"Thank you, Dr. Freud."

"Would you like to be twenty again?"

"Not if I had to have Mari for a mother. No. I was married at twenty. I went off to college at eighteen, with my other blouse and skirt in a borrowed suitcase—the high school English teacher got me a scholarship. Big deal for a coal miner's daughter. She thought I was going to be a teacher. I thought so too."

"Then Bill Ollenfield came along."

"He was the first man who ever paid any attention to me. I thought I was in love."

"No coed dorms in those days."

"Good heavens, no. You got bounced out of school if you were even suspected of any hanky-panky. Now they have special classes in the high schools for expectant mothers. Two of the kids in my class went to St. Louis with a group, to go to the theater, and didn't come back. Stayed overnight at a hotel. The president of the college and the dean of women were at the depot to meet them, the next day. They got married and had three kids."

"There must have been a lot going on. Human nature doesn't change much."

Frances smiled reminiscently. "Well, that was the era of the rumble seat. The big thing was not to get caught."

All I ask, Erika said to the god she had stopped believing in at eleven, all I want is for her not to have any more problems. She's had enough. Let her learn to take it as it comes.

She was fairly sure her prayers wouldn't be answered.

TWENTY-SIX

Erika backed down from the stepladder. "Is that about right? We need a new star, this one's getting tacky."

"That's the star we bought our first Christmas together, remember? We hung it in the window because we didn't have a tree."

"You really like Christmas, don't you?"

"I admit it doesn't make sense, but it does sort of get to me. I was on that bus the other day, the one the driver decorates, and it was really nice. People seemed friendly, everyone was joking—you know. I guess I'm being enthused for both of us."

"When I was a child in Vienna, Christmas was for Christians. Of course I knew about it, some of my friends were Catholic, and we had Channukah—my mother wasn't very *fromm*, she didn't keep a kosher house, but we never thought much about our Jewishness until we were reminded." She smiled wryly. "She did make a seder at Passover, my brother asked the questions."

Frances patted her hand. "I'm sorry I brought all this up."

Erika looked past her at their morning landscape: mulberry tree, cacti, palm tree. The swordlike leaves of the agave glittered in the sunlight. Along the rim of the patio a row of clay pots held candles planted in sand. Lighted after dark, they would flicker like fireflies. "There aren't any fireflies here. Nor dandelions. I miss dandelions."

"What brought that up?"

"The lumenaria."

"Oh. What are you doing this afternoon?"

"Mitchell called a briefing session, damn him. To get us used to the new equipment. I thought about looking in on the campus rally, can you imagine gays coming out as a group for

160

justice in Central America? Why, did you want to go somewhere?"

"Too bad to lose your day off."

"At least we'll get half a day. If Reagan has his way they'll
probably have to cut staff—that means more work and less
pay. Of course I could retire and give the kids a chance."

"If Reagan's cuts go through they'll need you more than
ever."

"Well, we're partly funded by the Feds, partly by the state,
partly by patient fees, and partly by those elegant ladies who
put on the fashion show every year. We couldn't lose all of it.
But if I did leave I wouldn't just sit around. Marty's talking
about starting a free clinic, paramedic kind of deal where people could get the standard tests and be referred to doctors and
hospitals—volunteer professionals, of course. Do you know
how many people in this town have no medical care at all? I
don't think they will stop Medicare, too many votes at stake,
but it's not much good if you don't have private insurance to
back it up."

"What's the campus rally?"

"El Salvador mostly. Gay rights are involved in it too, some
way. There's talk of cutting back on funding for organizations
that even mention the subject—not advocate it, but mention
it. The lesbians and gay men are coming out as a group."

Erika said seriously, "I'm a little tired of standing on the
sidelines and watching the young demonstrate. I just might go.
I just might carry a sign, or something."

"If anyone carries a sign it better be me. Do you realize
that I've reached optional retirement age? I could get eighty
percent of my Social Security if I quit working tomorrow? God,
that makes me feel old."

"I like you old. Not so young myself."

"That's nice. I don't have to worry about you leaving me
for an eighteen-year-old. It's a load off my mind."

The tree in the dining room stood tall and proud, glittering
with tinsel and covered with baubles collected over the last
twenty-five years. "Where does time go?" Erika wondered. Why
do things last so long, when people are so frail? She shivered.

"Cold?"

"A little tired, maybe. I may make a big pot of soup for supper—I don't feel very ambitious."

I'll be glad when the holidays are over, Erika told herself as Frances' little car pulled out of the drive and disappeared down the street. Too much fancy food, too many late nights, too much nostalgia, too much sense of time passing, all culminating in bad temper and viral infections. Why not ignore the whole thing? But you couldn't. There were Christmas cards to open—if you didn't send any, you had to write letters. Hilda in Oakland, Vince living in New York with a lover his own age, old pupils she didn't remember, the list was endless.

Suddenly she wanted to be out of the house. Her little blue Datsun stood in the drive, a good little car almost identical with the first one they had owned except that it had cost almost twice as much. Professionals, what with the escalating inflation, belonged to the new poor: but a car was a necessity here. They had an equity in the house, she reminded herself; they had enough to eat, the kind of clothes their jobs called for, a small savings account in case of emergency. Nothing to complain about. But a vague depression weighed her down.

She put on her sandals and locked the door behind her.

It was almost two, the hour set for the rally—that meant it might begin by half-past, demonstrations never started on time—you could count on being sunburned and tired before the guitar players showed up. It was seventy-five degrees, still incredible for December. Tree lights twinkled in windows, and along the curbs the palm trees stood tall and stately. Must look like this in Israel, Erika thought, fitting the Datsun into a parking space near a cluster of students who were erecting a makeshift platform. It was the Christmas break; the campus was almost deserted. Only a dozen bicycles in the long rack. She was not sure how much good political demonstrations did; perhaps it was like preaching to the choir, but she found herself hoping that this one would go well.

These kids hadn't been born when her contemporaries marched through the south for civil rights. They had never heard of Kent State, and mention of the Berrigans brought blank looks.

The movement had to be re-invented every ten years or so—these kids knew about Karen Silkwood but had never heard of Joe Hill, the Vietnam War was back there in the past somewhere. We could save time by bridging the generation gap, she thought irritably. As far as gay rights were concerned, this year's college students had invented the whole thing.

Two thin, bearded boys in tacky jeans, and a plump girl came up with armloads of posters. One of them said. "Hi, Miss Frohmann. Are you here for the rally? Do you want to say a few words?"

"Not this time, but I'll carry a sign."

Now why in heaven's name had she said that? It was a dull season for news. The television crews might be out, the campus newspaper would almost surely cover anything that was going on, and with any luck at all tomorrow's issue would have a group photo and a few misquotations from the speakers. Too late now. She leaned against the fountain base, noticed that one of the boys was nailing notices to a palo verde tree —no ecologists here—and the other had taken a banjo from the heap of posters and was trying a few notes.

Eight or nine others drifted in together. An older man showed up, a teacher perhaps, bearded and trim in khaki shorts and Birkenstocks. Then her attention was caught by a young woman in a Save the Seals tee shirt, and everything else dropped out of her mind. This was Frances at twenty—she had never seen a youthful picture of her lover but she recognized every feature. This was the Frances Kirby who had gone off to college with a borrowed suitcase. Never mind that the girl was self-assured and had plainly always been privileged. There was no room for doubt.

And the kid was headed straight for her.

"I don't think I know you. Are you going to speak?"

Politician's daughter, all right. Easy with people, a handshaker. Erika shook her head. One of the boys said, "This is Miss Frohmann. She's a school principal." She couldn't tell from his voice whether this put her on the other side or whether, just possibly, he was glad to have some support from the middle-class and respectable, not to mention the aging.

"I'm Isabel Ollenfield. I think it's so neat the way we're getting organized."

And you expect the revolution a week from Thursday, Erika thought crossly. Isabel didn't sound like Frances, her voice was higher and very clear. Sings soprano. She went on, "Are you a dyke?"

It's her business? And when did that word stop being an insult? "Yes, I am." Erika Frohmann, you have gone out of your mind.

"That's wonderful. Maybe you'd come and talk to my affinity group some time. We don't know many older women."

She isn't really trying to be rude, Erika admonished herself, and she isn't really trying to get me fired. "When does this rally start?"

"About half an hour ago." And that was what Frances would have said — must be something in heredity after all.

A young man carrying a guitar strolled across a patch of grass and sat down on the ground near them. Isabel ignored him. "Do you have a lover?"

"At my advanced age?" Erika gave her a look any classroom troublemaker would have recognized, and heard herself saying, "I've lived with your grandmother almost thirty years."

Now what in hell was happening to her? I'm possessed by demons. I need a good analyst. I've flipped.

Isabel's eyes widened. "But my grandmother lives in Park Ridge, Illinois, with my grandfather."

"I'm talking about your father's mother."

"Grandmother Ollenfield? She died a long time ago."

Erika tried to visualize Frances as Grandmother Ollenfield, and failed completely. "No, she left her husband. Is that what they told you, that she was dead?"

"They never talk about her." Isabel looked stricken. "It's so strange. I can't believe it."

Anger rose in Erika, whether for herself or for Frances she didn't know. With it came an amazing sense of freedom, of lightness. She said coldly, "You can check it out. Here, I'll give you the address and phone number." She tore a page from her pocket memo book, wrote hastily, and handed it to Isabel. Then she walked quickly to the Datsun and got in, leaving Isabel staring after her.

TWENTY-SEVEN

"I still don't know why I did it."

"Curiosity," Frances suggested. "You wanted to see how she'd react. Or how I would react."

Erika shook her head. "If I'd thought about that I'd have kept my mouth shut. I didn't think about anything—it was like being possessed. I was knocked out by seeing you reincarnated. And you know I've felt guilty for a long time—why I'm not out, how does someone with my lifestyle come out? We keep opening the closet door a crack and then scuttling back in and slamming it shut again."

"You were out when we met."

"I went back in when I started teaching again. I know what I am and feel good about it. If other people can't take it, that's their problem—that's the way the kids figure it. And they're right, but it is late in the day for us to change. Generation gap."

"It's not that simple."

"It's always been simple, only people kept complicating it. The way people make love is their own business."

"Does it help to stick your neck out?"

"It seems to, a little anyway. Look at Elaine Noble—she got elected. Look at Mattachine. Look at the lesbian mothers who are getting to keep their kids—Lili, for one."

Frances said, "I thought Isabel might want to get acquainted. I wasn't going to lean on her. After all, she was curious to come and meet me. Not that she showed much interest—she was polite, very polite. That was what, the twentieth? Thursday—Christmas was on Sunday."

"She brought a present. Give her credit, her mother has taught her some manners."

"That was five months ago."

165

"Well, she has her own life to live. Most college-age kids would never see their grandmothers if they weren't pressured into it."

"I don't feel much like a grandmother."

"You haven't had much practice."

Frances got up, moving a little stiffly, and began clearing the table. "When did she say she was coming?"

"Around eight. That could mean any time, I suppose."

"If I were a real grandmother I'd probably have baked a pie instead of leaving it to Sara Lee."

"Sara Lee does it better," Erika said unkindly but truthfully.

Frances turned back from the doorway. "Do you mind if I say I'm scared? I don't know what of."

"Being rejected by a baby dyke."

"Very funny."

The doorbell sounded, two short, clear notes. Frances hurried into the kitchen. Erika got up and walked slowly through the living room, switching on lights as she went.

Erika was in jeans and a halter; this wasn't going to be a formal visit. Or were the young ever formal, these days? Probably congressmen's wives had no more influence on the dress and behavior of their young than any other mothers. Erika produced what she hoped was a hospitable expression. "Come on in. Fran's in the kitchen making coffee."

"Would she mind if I had herb tea, if you have any? I'm off caffeine."

"Probably a good idea. Fran, make it camomile. Are you a vegetarian too?"

Isabel looked guilty. "I agree with it philosophically, but I still eat meat."

"That's about where we are. Come on inside where it's cool."

"I've been up a mountain with some kids. I grew up in flat country — the mountains are so beautiful."

Good at small talk, too. All the social graces. Raised to be a prom queen. What a blow for her mother. Unless of course she takes another girl to the prom. Like those two nice boys who were on TV.

Frances came in carrying a tray. Isabel sat down on the davenport and accepted a cup and small plate. "Something is different."

"We had the davenport upholstered. It was our Christmas gift to the house."

"What a neat idea. I guess I was a little nervous when I was here before."

"We're a little nervous too," Erika said bluntly. Frances, still standing, still holding the tray, seemed to have swallowed her tongue. Erika said, "I hope you're not off sugar too. That's real whipped cream."

"Gosh, it looks wonderful. I guess I worked off enough calories coming down from the mountains—did you know down is harder than up?" Isabel took a large appreciative bite, glad to have something to do. We could go on like this all night, Erika thought. She stood up and took the tray from Frances, pushing her down gently into the wing chair.

Isabel said in a hurry, "I went home last weekend. I don't go very often because so much is going on and she always wants me to stay over till Monday morning, and then something or other comes up and she reads the riot act, but I wanted to get something off my mind." She looked at Frances, tearing her gaze away from the pie as though the transition hurt. "I finally came out to them. I've been dying to do it ever since I knew about myself. Finally made it."

Frances was silent. Erika asked, "How did they take it?"

"Dad blew his top. He doesn't do that very often— Grandfather Ollenfield is the screamer in the family, but this time, wow!" Through the daze of tension Frances realized that Grandfather Ollenfield was Bill. Ridiculous, she thought. Isabel, uncorked, rushed on. "Dad doesn't give a damn about me. All he cares about is getting votes. I think he has his eye on some kind of federal appointment, now the Republicans are in. He wants me to stay in the closet another thirty or forty years."

"How about your mother?"

"Mother's always up to the minute on social issues," Mari's daughter said with a hint of bitterness. "It's a phase I'm going through. She thinks it's nice to be tolerant—but not where her own daughter is concerned, of course. It's like marrying a Black, okay for other people. Do I want to see a psychiatrist, she wanted to know."

"And?"

"I've seen one. She's a lesbian."

"That won't make much of an impression on your parents."

"So I'm not going home for a while, till they simmer down. Till they're ready to be reasonable." Isabel set her cup and well-scraped plate on a small table and turned towards her grandmother. "That isn't why I came here—I just thought you might like to know. So now Gay Pride Week is coming up and we're planning the biggest rally so far. They had a picnic last year but I wasn't here for it." She leaned forward. "Will you speak? We need somebody older—somebody who remembers how it was in the old days, when they were femme and butch, and the cops raided the bars, and all that. We want people to know we've been around for a while, we didn't just suddenly materialize out of nowhere—hell, we had Gertrude Stein and Jeannette Foster back in the Depression."

"Sappho," Erika murmured.

"Yes, and Ruth in the Bible! Will you do it?"

Frances spoke for the first time since the girl had come into the house. "Are you sure you're not doing this to get even with your parents?"

"Pretty sure. I thought about it. I talked it over with Dr. Settlemeyer. I'd rather not hurt them, but I won't hide. I won't."

Erika said, "It's bad enough for your father to have a gay daughter. A gay mother might kill him politically."

"That's his problem."

Erika said, "I suppose it might get him some gay votes, if it comes to that."

Frances moved in the chair. "Whose side are you on, his or hers?"

"Yours," Erika told her. "And mine. Bob was old enough to get married when you came out. He owes you something.

He owes himself something, if it comes to that. A little honesty, a little insight."

They were silent for a moment. Isabel looked from one to the other. They could hear a dog barking down the street. The Air Force couple next door, a new pair this year, slammed a car door. The kitchen faucet dripped, stopped. and dripped again.

Frances said slowly. "I think I'll do it. I think it's time. Not for her sake, nor for Bob's, but for myself." She looked at Isabel. "How long would you want me to talk?"

"About fifteen minutes. Just little things — how we work with the guys now. Well, that's not a little thing, but you know what I mean."

Erika said suddenly, "No one's consulted me about this."

"It's her decision," Isabel said, surprised. "Her — I don't know what to call you."

"Frances will do. I'm a little old to start being a grandma."

"We're a family," Erika said implacably. "If she's going to speak, I'm going to be on the platform. Moral support."

"Your job is more sensitive than mine," Frances objected.

"I can retire if I have to. Or I can go to court." Now Erika seemed to be enjoying this. "All I'm saying is, it's time for me too."

Isabel looked at each of them. "Maybe you ought to talk it over." But they had been communicating, apparently, in some way she wasn't aware of. Frances got up and came to stand beside Erika, looking down at her with an expression Isabel had never seen on anyone else's face. "You're right. We'll both be there."

"Are you sure you want to do it?"

Frances said, "We are real sure. I don't want to hurt anyone's feelings, Isabel, but this is something we need to do. Not for you and not for the movement. For ourselves."

Isabel got up, looking uncertain. "Well, I'll tell the committee—"

No one saw her leave. Nobody said goodbye.

They had forgotten that she was there.

———

Books From Banned Books

Ripening,
Valerie Taylor $8.95
These Lovers Fled Away,
Morgan Graham $8.95
Profiles Encourage (Nonfiction),
Pamela S. Johnson $8.95
Like Coming Home: Coming-Out Letters (Nonfiction),
Edited by Meg Umans $7.95
A Herd of Tiny Elephants,
Stan Leventhal $8.95
Dairy of a New York Queen,
William Barber $8.95
gay(s)language,
H. Max $4.95
Kite Music,
Gary Shellhart $8.95
Mountain Climbing in Sheridan Square,
Stan Leventhal $8.95
Skiptrace,
Antoinette Azolakov $8.95
A Cry in the Desert,
Jed A. Bryan $9.95
Cass and the Stone Butch,
Antoinette Azolakov $8.95
Dreams of the Woman Who Loved Sex,
Tee Corinne $7.95
Tangled Sheets,
Gerard Curry $7.95
Death Strip,
Benita Kirkland $8.95
Days in the Sun,
Drew Kent $8.95
Fairy Tales Mother Never Told You,
Benjamin Eakin $5.95
The Gay of Cooking Cookbook,
The Kitchen Fairy $10.95

These books are available from your favorite bookstore or by mail from:

Banned Books
Number 231, P.O. Box 33280, Austin, Texas 78764

Add $1.50 postage and handling for one (1) book. For more than one book, add 10% of order total. Texas residents, please also add 8% sales tax. Send your name and address for our free current catalog and to be added to our mailing list.